ZORBA THE BUDDHA

Spineless Wonders
ABN98156041888
PO Box 220 STRAWBERRY HILLS
New South Wales, Australia, 2012
www.shortaustralianstories.com.au

First published as ebook by Spineless Wonders 2020
Reproduced as paperback in 2021

Text copyright © Katerina Cosgrove 2020
Cover design by Bettina Kaiser.
Edited by Jess Magrath. Layout by Heike Krieger. Publishing
assistant Timothy Stephen Smith.

Typeset in Adobe Garamond Pro
Printed and bound by Lightning Source Australia

National Library of Australia
Zorba The Buddha /Katerina Cosgrove
1st ed.
ISBN 978-1-925052-65-7 (pbk.)
ISBN 978-1-925052-56-5 (ebk.)A823.4

A catalogue record for this
book is available from the
National Library of Australia

This project has been assisted by the Copyright Agency
Cultural Fund.

ZORBA THE BUDDHA

KATERINA COSGROVE

Contents

Preface

The search for meaning in spiritual teachings beyond the scripts and dogmas of organised western religion and its churches has a long history. Over recent centuries many teachers and masters, good and bad, have sought new forms of ideation and practice to present to the world's seekers – not least the vast numbers who have fled their 'birth' creeds and the myriads of the soul-sick – as a means to peace and enlightenment. One of the more interesting episodes in this history concerns Bhagwan Rajneesh, who was both principal agent and subject of a movement that experienced a spectacular rise and fall in the 1980s.

The story of *Zorba the Buddha* centres on the years 1984-86 and an attempt to build a further ashram for Rajneesh and followers on Crete, Greece after a then-recent disaster in Oregon, USA. In taking the creative liberty to imagine or reimagine the Rajneeshi story in those years, in focusing on the contradictory and complex character of Rajneesh, his multifarious thoughts and wishes at a time of great stress, as well as the inner lives and roles of various acolytes, believers and manipulators, the author has given us here a most fascinating rendition of that dramatic episode.

Writing plausible prose fiction that is sourced in history but not weighed down by it is no easy matter, weaker exercises are often mired in the quotidian or leave some tell-tale taste of phoniness or uncertainty. But that most definitely isn't the case with *Zorba the Buddha*. Katerina Cosgrove has succeeded in taking material that, in poorer hands, might have become low-grade social satire or black comedy and lifted it to another, more worthy level entirely.

This is an ambitious and richly imagined piece – and in the accompanying synopsis and essay an open-hearted and revealing one. We are generously given access to the author's own interests and yearnings, where among other things she presents her personal engagement with questions of how to live and be in the world, at the same time as she creatively measures one eventually doomed attempt to deliver on those questions. She convincingly suggests that at a certain period there was at the heart of the Rajneeshi movement a genuine desire to develop a new kind of liberation, rather more than any desire to spread fantasy talk for the purpose of cult-building.

From the intensely personalised relationships among a group of central followers to the naivete and foolishness displayed by its worst actors, the author captures the hermetic nature of the Rajneesh enterprise along with its incapacity to recognise and deal with brutal, real-world authority. In all, Katerina Cosgrove gives us characters who are utterly believable, whether in their conduct of reprehensible power-plays, or in their poignancy as ordinary, suffering human beings diminished by life's defeats and losses.

Angelo Loukakis

August 2020

Zorba the Buddha

BHAGWAN

AGHIOS NIKOLAOS, CRETE, 1986

Late winter sun makes sleepy mudras behind my eyelids. My fingers and toes tingle, my stiff spine unravels as I sit more deeply in the chair. I hurt. I ache. But I am content, in a state of bliss. One with the world: with this cracked and worn cow's leather, slippery and hot under my thighs, the beauty and silence and terror of that beast's dying, the smell of olive trees and pine resin and diesel fuel off the Aegean, this morning beam of sunlight which hits me right in the forehead, a third eye. This is not meditation. This is a dentist's chair, and I am high on gas.

One of the Australian journalists looks down at my manicured toes. Is he showing respect or merely bored? When he arrived at the villa and caught his first glimpse of me, I heard him say to his compatriots in that squawking upside-down parrot voice, 'Geez, he looks like God incarnate!'

I begin to speak. 'Esoteric means bullshit,' I say, and his eyes widen. 'I piss on sacred cows – and not just the Indian ones.'

This gets a laugh from all of them: from the journalists and sound crew and cameramen, even from Devamarga and Krishna and Vishva. I like telling jokes. Laughter wakes people up more surely than any amount of OMing or posturing.

The journalist settles back on his heels and the cameras roll.

'So, Bhaghwan Rajneesh, do you miss the Rolls Royces?'

'No, do you?'

He tries again.

'They also call you the sex guru.'

I cut him off with a sharp gesture of my hand and turn to the next journalist: younger, scruffy, shy.

'Do you have anything of substance to say?'

He squirms. 'Ah, what do you think of the attitude of the Greek government toward you? They've offered you the hospitality of their country. Are you grateful?'

I pierce him with a baleful eye – I still know how to do that.

'Two things.' I hold up the fingers of my right hand. 'Number one: Greek Orthodox religion is smoke and mirrors and Greek priests are idiots and donkeys. We don't care what the government thinks, what the bishop thinks. And they are already thinking stupid things. Number two: Greek people are parochial, narrow-minded. Patriotism is the absurd refuge of the ignorant.'

'So, you won't be staying here long, Bhagwan?'

'As long as they don't make me drink hemlock, I will stay. But to me, without Socrates, Greece is nothing. We have plans to open an ashram on one of the islands. Many sannyasins will come here. Millions. At this very moment they are celebrating my arrival, dancing in the tavernas and on the streets.'

'Do you have any Cretans among your followers?'

'Not yet. They are drugged by the poison of their religion. My God! Can't they recognise me?'

He looks away, baffled. I train my eyes on him and he comes back, dazed.

'I am the same person they poisoned twenty-five centuries ago. They have forgotten me, but I have not forgotten them. Do you know who I am?'

They both shake their heads, the uneducated bastards. They think I'm crazy. The older one barks at me.

'And your commune in Oregon, Bhagwan? Is it finished?'

I dismiss him with a wave of my hand. Vishva knows the cue. She comes forward, motioning them away. All at once, I am tired. I want to enjoy my first nitrous oxide of the day alone. I want to look through the circular window of my sitting room at an icy sea I can't ever hope to immerse myself in. I can smell the toxic fumes of the oils and perfumes on all of them, the shampoos and gels and balms.

'Go away!'

The older journalist jumps up, knocking into his colleagues.

'Go away, shower and put on fresh clothes if you wish to see me again.'

When they're gone, Vishva gives me my Valium. As always, she presents it to me on a little round silver tray, inlaid with mother-of-pearl. A shining white pill, like the promise of enlightenment.

Did I say I was enlightened? You must have heard wrong.

*

MUKUNDA

AGHIOS NIKOLAOS, CRETE, 1986

So many of us come. I left my daughters in our drab, brown-wallpapered London apartment and flew to Heraklion as soon as I got the fax. It said 'Come Be with Bhagwan Shree' – and after all the shit I had to put up with in Rajneeshpuram, after the fights and bitching and fears for my life, I felt as if the red-type words were addressed to me. Only me. I was the one who found the Cretan villa for Him. I was the one who organised the new furniture and Turkish rugs and expensive linen, all the little things I knew He liked. It was my director friend's holiday house, and even though he'd never met Bhagwan, he was happy to do a favour for me.

My eldest, Eleni, tried to stop me from going, saying He was a charlatan, He'd already taken all our money, our social standing, the regard of the shipping community, the trust of our London-Greek relatives and friends. She refused to be called Vashti any longer, now we had gone home. I told her she wasn't worthy of coming to Greece, after all her negativity.

But I did bring Shakti with me. He begged to come.

When I got here, three hundred other sannyasins had already arrived within the week. Now they're crammed into spare rooms and on rooftops in Greek houses, hotels, pensions, sleeping on the beach. At night, they drink tsikoudia and retsina and break plates and dance to the Zorba sirtaki. I don't join them.

I walk up to the gate of His villa and demand to be let in. I wait out there, in the midday sun, until it sets behind the mountains. My familiar Greek landscape reminds me a little of our Oregon ranch then – arid peaks, dusty and grey, devoid of vegetation. Kazantzakis called the Cretan countryside ordered and restrained, like good prose. Maybe he was thinking of somewhere else, not this sombre, craggy hillside. I see no order here. Instead, I see the memories of all our failures. I sit on the ground, feeling the tentative warmth of the day seep away from me and a dead chill rise from the earth.

Then the guards say He is ready to see me. I feel such relief; it's like the early days of our love. I exist just for Him – and Him for me. I pass through enclosed courtyards of carob and olive trees, bees swaying drunken through blossoms of tamarisk. I'm in Nirvana, even before I set eyes on Him.

'Ah, Ma Yoga Mukunda,' He says, as soon as I enter the room. 'My freedom girl is not so free these days, eh?'

As soon as I hear Him speak, I remember how sad I am. Sad that He is not, and never will be, as I imagine Him. He will never be the young guru I encountered as a girl in His Indian garden, with love in His eyes for every flower, every blade of grass, the dappled light playing on His hands – and for me. That love does not exist anymore.

Ma Yoga Vishva laughs. She sits in the shadow of His dentist's chair, cross-legged. She hands Him a glass of wine. The last rays of light illuminate the garnet-coloured liquid, her saffron-reddish robes, the outlines of her nipples, the chunky gold and diamond bracelets on her wrists, twins to the ones He wears. She flashes me a look of pity and triumph. I know He is referring to the boy. How He knows Shakti is here with me, I have no idea. He always sensed everything about me – the shame, the striving, the dissembling, the untouched radiance beneath. But I'm in my late forties now and will no longer be spoken to like this.

I open my mouth to say something, but He stops me with His hand. There is a force emanating from His open palm, all blue and purple like an uncut amethyst. I can feel it boring into my forehead, but not yet into my heart. This heart of mine is limp, a landed fish. There have been too many promises not kept, too many disappointments. Too much pain, for all of us. I'm not sure what I believe anymore.

He sees I'm not wearing His colours, or the mala around my neck with his image. I gave that up as soon as He left the ranch, put them on again for a few weeks in London, then discarded them forever. It was too hard. My daughters wouldn't go anywhere with me if I wore them. My extended family crossed the street to avoid me.

Vishva fingers her own mala, absently, humming under her breath. She ignores me now, as if I don't exist.

He points to His white hair and beard, then in an elegant gesture to my head. I used to dye my waist-length hair black every three weeks, keeping the silver halo at bay. When He stopped, so did I.

I kneel at His feet, but don't bow my head. I look up at His face as He smooths down his long beard with both hands, the same movement I've seen him make caressing a Persian cat or a woman's body.

'You can see my beard now. Is it greyer than when you last saw me? It has become grey so quickly because I have lived so intensely in the past few months, I have compressed almost two hundred years in fifty.'

'Bhagwan?' I venture. He nods. 'Will you be staying here? I mean, in Greece? Shall I try and find a good spot for a retreat centre, a commune?'

He smiles. When He does so, His eyes light up, as full of life as I remember them in the early days in Pune. When He stops, and His face is once again in repose, I am saddened. It's as if He's no longer there.

'Yes. You are Greek, you know how to speak to these people. Give them money, give them cigarettes, give them gold watches. Bribe them. Cajole them. Promise them. Lie to them, if you must. But make sure you find me a place with sunshine, trees, flowers and water. All those things she failed to find.'

I know He is referring to Sharabo. I make as if to get up and again He stops me with an open palm.

'And remember, Mukunda. If you don't tell me every little thing you are doing, I will still know, okay?'

*

SHAKTI

AGHIOS NIKOLAOS, CRETE, 1986

I never had that thing they rave about called darshan. I didn't touch Bhagwan's feet, didn't get all wobbly and pass out. Maybe it's a girl thing. I got my new name through Mukunda and that was it. I never saw what she calls the vision of the divine. The master's light is snuffed out for me. I want to go home.

Why she's brought me all this way I have no idea. She thinks I wanted to come. I pretended I was all excited about going with her, because I knew that if I told her the truth, she'd be jealous. Jealous of her own daughters. I was happy hanging out in London with her two girls, smoking hash in the evenings, watching Hollywood action movies. Sometimes we'd go out at night, to a club. Mukunda didn't come with us even once; she went to bed so early. She would give me the side-eye, the dirty looks. Fuck me if I was going to go to sleep at nine, just like those crazy days at the commune. I didn't need to wake up for anything in London. Not back-breaking work, not meditation, not quick morning sex.

Since we've left the commune Mukunda and me don't have sex anymore. We don't even sleep in the same bed. Here in Greece, in the master's villa, we sleep in twin beds on opposite sides of the room. Hard as boards, starched white sheets with hospital corners. She tells me the master doesn't approve of our relationship, but I think that's just an excuse. It's like she's gone off me ever since I had the snip. But she was the one who convinced me to do it.

We were in the shitty hole of a room assigned to us on the Oregon ranch. Shaky thin plasterboard walls that didn't even reach the ceiling, separating us from the other workers. You could hear everything, just like living in a toilet cubicle.

'Shakti.' She took my head in both her hands. 'You're a sannyasin now. You're no longer a little boy called Homer Miller. Do you remember what sannyas means? Lay it all down. Renounce everything, even yourself. Lay it all at His feet. He knows what to do with it.'

I turned away in that narrow, noisy bed, so that my back was to her. She leaned over and whispered into my ear.

'Leave the past behind, Shakti. Leave your self behind. There is no self, not anymore. You know what I did when I took sannyas? I burned my photos, donated all my money, forgot about my family. Nobody has called me by my birth name since then.'

I changed position, lay on my back staring up at the ceiling – low, covered in the squashed black carcasses of mosquitoes from the previous summer. 'What is your birth name? I never asked you.'

'It doesn't matter.'

'Come on, tell me. I really want to know.'

'Okay. It's Kalliope. The lovely-voiced muse, in Ancient Greek.'

'That's real pretty. Better than Mukunda. Mukunda sounds like something you get stuck in your throat.'

'Very funny. Try not to change the subject. So, what do you think? Are you a sannyasin or not?'

I said nothing. She kissed me on the forehead. I closed my eyes.

'Well?' She shook me, hard. 'He says you have to. It's nothing to do with me.'

I flounced over until we were laying close, eye to eye. Her breath stank of pot.

'Why don't you get it done? You've had three kids already, you're old.' Here my voice broke, and I kicked myself. 'I'm only eighteen! What if I want to have a kid someday?'

She smoothed the hair back over my forehead like my mam used to when I was small, traced the down on my chin and cheekbones with one finger.

'Shh, Shakti, it's going to be okay. Everything will be okay. Just do it. You make yourself suffer by thinking too hard. He knows. He knows the past and the present and the future. If He tells you to do it, He knows what's good for you, now and forever.'

I got it done the next day. It didn't hurt much, afterward. The ranch doctors and nurses were so kind. I ate special food. I didn't have to go to work for three days, though I missed the hens and beef cattle. I hoped the others were looking after them properly, what with the snow and all.

But when I got better and could feel the energy rising in me like the coiled jewel serpent the sannyasins always talk about, I ran out into the sage and juniper trees where I could be alone. I sat at the base of a trunk, reached into my jeans and touched the two tiny wounds on either side of my balls. I pressed my face to the smooth, chocolate-coloured bark and cried. I must have cried for a long time.

When I stopped, the forest was dark. I went for a long walk away from the shelter of the trees, getting colder and colder. The coyote carcasses killed by the local farmers – people like my pa – hung from barbed-wire fences, stiff with rigor mortis and ice crystals.

I felt like a dead coyote myself, hollowed out and rigid with regret.

*

BHAGWAN and SHARABO

Villa Galini, Aghios Nikolaos, Crete

February 1986

Ma Anand Sharabo,

You ask me to forgive you. How can I? You did not commit crimes against me, but against everyone in the ashram. I have told you before. I do not forgive you and I will never forgive you. I don't even know why I read your letter, or why I am replying. You have lost my trust and once trust is lost; pure love also becomes impossible.

But you are right, as you often were. If you want to experience Hell, visit America. Your little joke rings true, at least for me. You turned a meditation camp into a concentration camp.

How many letters do they allow you to send? I expect you're also writing to lawyers, journalists, publishers. I know you; you won't let this opportunity go to waste.

Let me tell you why I cannot forgive you. In your haste to gain my praise and respect, you chose the wrong site for our Buddha-field. You chose a dusty, barren wasteland. A desert. A place where it was a furnace for two months of the year and the rest of the time ice age upon ice age. You made life miserable for me. And I blame only you, nobody else. Not your little gang of fascists, not your temple mums. Only you.

I told you when we got there, as soon as it got cold and dark. I said, 'Sharabo, I am having great difficulty staying in my body in this place. My ship is waiting.' Your solution? To buy me more cars. More watches, more jewellery, more hand-knitted woollen caps to cover my poor head. I was suffocated under all those useless objects. They did not help me stay in my body; they took me even further away.

Let me tell you this, which I have learned from Zorba. The highest point of our existence is not in gaining knowledge, which you, Sharabo, always had. It is also not victory, which you constantly strived for, at all costs. Nor is it even virtue or goodness – those dull, meaningless expressions of Christianity. It is an even greater peak we scale, that of sacred awe. If you had ever felt this in my presence, even once, even for a mere instant, things would not have deteriorated the way they did.

Sharabo, you call me a rascal guru; you say all I ever gave you was crazy wisdom. But crazy wisdom is the only antidote to crazy times. I embody dark and light, chaos and calm, creation and destruction. I am everything, and I am no-thing. I am nothing.

And I say this to you again – I am an empty mirror. If you come to me angry, you see anger in me. If you come to me sad, you see tears glistening in my eyes. If you come to me horny, all you see is lust in me.

It's all up to you. What did you see, Sharabo? Ego, pride, despair? Selfishness. Because you are selfish, you saw only selfishness in me.

Don't write to me again. Vishva will throw any letters from you on the fire, where they belong.

Your Master,

Bhagwan Shree Rajneesh

*

Federal Correction Institution, Dublin, California

February 1986

Bhagwan,

I cannot sleep. You told me once that if I ever left your side you would haunt me in my dreams. I have no dreams at all now, yet you haunt me when I lay awake on this lumpy mattress, when I do my pitiful laundry, when I move a forkful of this food – like sour cat vomit – to my mouth.

My mouth is hungry for forgiveness. It cries out at night, untouched by your fingers, by your grace. I loved you. I chose the devotional path, the way of bhakti yoga. You told me it was the only way to know you, to be in a true love affair with the master.

You call me selfish all the time now. Once, you loved my selfishness.

'I teach selfishness.' I heard you say it, over and over, in your discourses. I even heard you in my sleep, as I napped at the foot of the dais, under your feet. But I was not selfish.

I was selfless, for you. Everything I did was for you: your wellbeing, your safety, your life. I had no life of my own. Now you have pushed me away and I am a broken doll, limp and flattened.

Is this your new sadhana for me? Is this the cruel device you're using now to break me utterly?

Please reply. I am in agony.

Your servant,

Ma Anand Sharabo

*

BHAGWAN

RAJNEESHPURAM, OREGON, 1984

No hope for other than what is. I repeat it in my head. No hope for other than what is. This is my current mantra. Even with this comfort, a metronome under my breath, a lighted votive candle in my heart, I am sad and disappointed. I am country-less, homeless. She showed me photographs of a lush wilderness, streams of running water under trees as tall as skyscrapers. She promised that I would walk among them. And where did she bring me? To this godforsaken desert, where frost crunches under my fur-lined boots and I shiver in my light Indian robes.

I am in despair. In prison – the prison of her love and care. The snow-light hurts my eyes. I can no longer write letters or read. I live in a darkened room. My eighty thousand books still in boxes, unpacked. I, who would read ten or more books per day, can read nothing. I can do nothing. I have vowed not to speak.

Devamarga, my doctor, flits around me like an awkward ghost. Vishva warms my cold bed at night and during my naps, chivvies our cook to make me delicacies that are unheard of here in America. She tries to work out what my grandmother would make for me when I was a little boy. She wheedles – 'What was your favourite treat, Master?' – and I can say nothing. I only shake my head. Here in Lao Tzu House, silence is supreme. We hear the massive flakes of snow falling on panes of glass, the far-off yells and jokes made by sannyasins building or laying pipes or driving tractors, sometimes the bass lowing of our dairy cows, shut up for winter. We are attuned to every shout, every whisper.

The only sounds I make are at my twice daily gas sessions, after my dentist, Krishna, seats me in the soft leather chair. My lower back is agony, my degenerative disc still unhealed – even here, in the place of drugs and surgery and medical miracles. I refuse to see any of their doctors or surgeons. I inhale the smell of dead cow and the sharp-sweet tang of chemicals. I sigh and close my eyes and the gas takes effect, making mandalas and pentagrams behind my brows. The words come. My book editor sits at my feet, legs tucked beneath her red velvet dress, and transcribes.

When Sharabo comes to me each morning for her ninety-minute darshan – 'work meeting', she calls it – I nod and smile and pat her fierce, wiry little hand. I have nothing else to give her. She wants nothing else. She already wears the power I have bestowed upon her like armour, like the Smith & Wesson revolver at her belt.

She tells me the newspapers here want to blame us for everything. The police are not interested in investigating the explosion of one of our hotels in Portland. They claim we did it ourselves, as a publicity stunt. Why then did only our own people become injured in the resulting fire?

She senses more trouble ahead from the Wasco county officials, the small-town mentality of the local Antelope farmers.

'Don't worry, Bhagwan,' she tells me. 'I don't believe in Jesus' way of turning the other cheek. I go for both cheeks.'

I have chosen Sharabo to be my secretary, to give you a little taste of what fascism really means.

*

MUKUNDA

AGHIOS NIKOLAOS, CRETE, 1986

I stay awake most nights here in Villa Galini, listening to Shakti breathe. I know he's not asleep either; he's usually a loud and restless sleeper, warm and snuffling, like a toddler with a cold. Now he's too still and quiet to be sleeping. He's thinking as hard as I am. Tonight, we repose in our white twin beds, on either side of this cold monk's cell of a room, far away from each other. A screech owl calls. I'm tempted to crawl into his cramped bed and take comfort from the sweet avidity of his teenage body, but I know he doesn't want me. He doesn't want me anymore.

At the Oregon ranch, Ma Anand Sharabo or Ma Yoga Vishva would come to wake me at four some mornings, for special darshan. I reluctantly untangled myself from Shakti's sticky, childish limbs and tried to suppress my scream at the moment my feet contacted the icy concrete floor.

I taught Shakti more about 'no-mind' during our orgasms together than any amount of meditation, sitting still and vainly trying to empty our heads of thought. My Master – He taught me these lessons, so I could pass them on to others. That's why I didn't protest at being woken at that hour, padding in my bedroom slippers across the frostbitten ground to Lao Tzu House, crawling without sound into His plush, curtained bed, recently warmed by Vishva's body. That's why I still went.

Shakti was jealous but I knew he was trying hard not to say anything. It was all so new to him. I told him there were very few monogamous couples on the ranch. That he and I were probably the only ones. I didn't count My Master as a lover. He was more like a fast-track, confusing encounter with the Divine. I tried to teach Shakti about the tantric acceptance of everything: no judgement, no restriction, no expectation. He looked at me as if I was speaking Ancient Greek. My Master called it indulgence with awareness:

The Total Way, not Buddha's Middle Way. I called it surrender.

I met Shakti in our Zorba the Buddha café in the little town of Antelope, when he was still called Homer Miller. I'd noticed a young boy always there in the afternoons, watching us as we ate and talked and laughed in our groups of four or five. I could see he was both fascinated and repelled by our long, unbrushed hair, the men's wild beards, our saffron and crimson and rose-coloured clothes, the swinging malas around our necks, with His face staring out of them.

The boy sat at the counter, sipping a soda. Week after week, he was there. I wondered if he was skipping school just to look at us. He would swivel on his stool, taking us in. He was scrubbed, clean-cut, his ears pinkly raw from too much hot water and soap. His short brown hair slicked back with some cheap gel, reeking of chemicals. I liked his broad, pale face, the sharp cheekbones, the long, gangly limbs he had no idea where to place. His eyes were pure, two polished green marbles. I knew that if I wanted him to join us, he'd have to ditch everything, including the soap and gel.

I used to be one of the best sniffers at the ashram in Pune. I would bend over in my watery silk robes, snuffling, loud as a truffle pig and delicate as a cat, at would-be sannyasins' armpits, at their hair and groins and the vulnerable crease at the back of their necks. My Master was so sensitive to odours that He couldn't bear anyone, even in a Buddha Hall of thousands, wearing a trace of perfume or essential oil or aftershave. He was like a honeybee, alert and sensitive to every molecule.

After about a month, I sidled up to the young boy at the counter. I sat close, so that my leg through the thin fabric of my trousers touched his. I paid for his drink and ordered a milky chai for myself. We were running the café now; no longer did it sell bacon or eggs or hot dogs. The aromas of cardamom and cumin perfumed the air. We served brown rice and beans and lentils, and not much else.

'Hey, boy,' I said. 'I've been watching you sitting here for weeks. Don't you have anywhere else to be? What's your game?'

'Well, golly,' he answered, putting on a Midwestern accent – or was that truly what he sounded like? 'It ain't a crime to sit in a diner in the afternoon and have a drink. What do you say, huh?'

'Hey, mother-gosher,' I said, mocking his voice. 'Are you a spy? Aren't you just as sick of us being here in your town, as all your cronies are, over there?'

I jerked my thumb at the farmers across the road, wide-legged, talking about us in their tight conspiratorial knots, their faded plaid shirts and wide-brimmed hats hiding any distinguishing features. Some men wore T-shirts under their plaid with the slogans Better Dead Than Red and Bag a Bhagwan. On the telegraph pole nearby, one of several printed handbills we tore down any time we saw them: Sex Guru Go Home.

The boy looked at me properly then. 'Why no,' he said. 'I mean, I'm not sure. You're not too bad.'

I laughed. 'Really? I bet your daddy doesn't think so.'

He looked down at his overly large hands, flat on the countertop.

'I don't care what Pa thinks.'

'Are you sure? Are you brave enough to tell him that? What if he never speaks to you again? What if he tells all your friends not to speak to you?'

'I told you, I don't care. I'm so glad you're all here. I've never seen anyone like you. I – I want to be just like you.'

The next day, he was at the ranch. His parents accused us of kidnapping him. The school and sports club and church got involved. But he had just turned eighteen the week before, so there was nothing they could do. Was it worth it for Homer Miller to turn his back on his mother and father and relatives and friends, on the very town he was born in? His culture, everything he'd known? You see, poor Shakti never got to dance all night with me, oiled and slick, glistening with jewels of sweat. He didn't get to hear My Master speak. He didn't experience kundalini or Mystic Rose. No sunrise Dynamic Meditations. No worshipping of the Divine.

Instead, we woke together in the pre-dawn darkness to worship at work for twelve-plus hours a day, seven days a week. Work was our new spirituality. I worshipped at dusting, cooking, sweeping, mopping. I worshipped until my hair was matted with grit and my nails turned black and ragged. I knew it was one of His elaborate devices: push us to intense self-observation, to exhaustion and epiphany. The attainment of freedom, somehow.

Shakti worshipped the Divine knee-deep in shit. He mucked out the barns, shovelled chicken manure and helped milk and muster the cows. He didn't know what had hit him. He lost weight. The only thing that kept him sane was my presence in our bed each night, my murmured promises that things would change, they would get better, we just needed time to establish the commune and then we could laugh, sing, dance and love until we burst.

But I was paranoid, like everyone else. Scared of what the locals would do to us, especially now we had stolen one of their own. They all owned guns. And in a sense, I was more frightened of what Sharabo was capable of doing to them in retaliation. Our 'peace force', in their incongruous pink and orange uniforms, ramped up their firearm training.

On my brief walks through the dirt-streaked snow to visit Shakti and his animals, to bring him a thermos of tea or a morsel I'd filched from the kitchens, I saw Air Force fighter jets from the naval base flying so low I could discern the faces of the pilots, anonymous behind their visors, stern and unblinking.

*

SHAKTI

RAJNEESHPURAM, OREGON, 1984

What was I expecting? A place with a swimming pool and naked ladies draped around it? Was I looking for some tropical paradise with palms and cocktails all over the place? Instead, I had broken, filthy fingernails and aching knees. I had a gaping wound under my chin, where I'd accidentally leaned on the shovel too hard and the handle had ricocheted up and hit me. Nobody checked if I was okay. Nobody gave me stitches. I got one pint of beer a day, after work. My ration was twenty cigs a day, which I could trade with the men for a bit more food. Mostly, they just got stolen.

But I had Mukunda. It was the first time I had ever had sex. That wonder alone – having access to her every night – made everything else worth it. And from what she told me about Bhagwan, he was nothing like the phony holy elders of Antelope, the minister and church ladies, the cruel teachers and even crueller coaches at my school. Bhagwan allowed everything. He wasn't hung up. Being in the commune made me feel as if I was right for the first time in my life. There was no guilt in our sex. We were free to do anything. We tasted each other. We dug our fingers and tongues and my cock into every nook and cranny. I was her and she was me.

There were no meditation groups at the ranch anymore, Mukunda told me. Everyone was too busy. But a couple of times a week she would take me to the encounter groups. In the beginning, I mostly sat in a corner and watched. People were screaming, fighting, kicking, crying. Some lay on the floor, pretending to be born out of the open thighs of the women, squalling and sucking. They were all naked.

Some would come out of there with bruises, black eyes, broken limbs. I didn't want any of that to happen to me. I had enough injuries from working with the animals, trying to grow food. I didn't need any new badges of participation.

After a couple of weeks, Mukunda said I should join in. She pulled off my clothes and led me into the circle. It was so dim in the room that all I could see were her large nipples in front of me, fuzzy and black, and the dark curly bushes of the women who hadn't shaved.

It freaked me out. I couldn't bear seeing her with anyone else and I was too scared to approach any of the other women. We stopped going. She said we could try again another time. That for now, I was enough for her.

But one night she sat on our bed wearing a flannel granny nightgown, with the buttons done up all the way to her neck.

'Shakti,' she whispered. 'You know about AIDS, don't you?'

I nodded. I felt a cold dread sink down into my groin and stay there.

'Do you – do I – have it?' I croaked.

She laughed.

'No, silly. It's just that Our Master is being hyper-vigilant. He doesn't want any of us getting sick.'

She flicked at the thin grey blanket with one hand and I saw what she'd been hiding under there. Three sets of rubber gloves, a packet of condoms.

'He says we all have to use these from now on.'

'Three sets of gloves?' I asked, incredulous. 'Why three?'

'That's what he says. Three sets every time we have sex.'

'That's crazy!' I shouted.

'Shh!' She brought her palm hard to my lips. 'Someone will hear you. Then we'll be sent away too.'

'What do you mean – too?'

'Sharabo has sent away anyone who's gay. She and Our Master are worried they could spread the disease among us.'

I looked at her, shocked. She groped at her buttons, drew her nightgown up over her head in one movement and her big, floppy breasts gleamed white in the gloom.

'Shall we try them, then?'

I wriggled out of my trousers and fell on top of her.

'Wait.' She made a scrunching sound as she took a pair of gloves out of the plastic packet.

'Put these on. And one more thing. No more oral or anal sex. He says so.'

I bent down to kiss her mouth and she jerked her head away.

'Hey. No kissing allowed either.'

*

SHARABO

Federal Correction Institution, Dublin, California

February 1986

Bhagwan, my beloved,

Do you remember the morning Ma Yoga Vishva and I had our worst fight? You didn't want to drink your milk. I had gone to the barn myself before dawn and supervised the milking of Your special cow, Summer. The boy Shakti was doing it expertly enough, truth be told.

I brought the lidded pewter jug to You myself, as I did every morning. I poured out the thin stream of fresh, raw milk into Your glass. And that morning You refused to touch it. I insisted. You shook Your head. I fetched a long-handled spoon.

'One spoonful, Bhagwan. Just one. You need to keep up your strength.'

You kept Your mouth clamped shut and looked away. It was then I knew they had done something to you. All those ones You lived with in Lao Tzu House. They had changed You and I feared for Your life.

'Leave him be,' Vishva said, from her position on the floor at Your feet. 'You're not his mother.'

I looked at her. 'You have always been his whore, I know that. But yes, I am his mother. I look after him as you never could.'

She got up and lunged at me with her nails out. I stepped back, shielding my eyes.

'You dare threaten me, wildcat! Get away before I damage you permanently!'

My hand went, unbidden, to the gun at my belt. She saw this and subsided. You pushed her down to Your feet again. Do You remember doing that?

'Vishva, be still,' You said. 'Look at Sharabo. Appreciate her. She is so beautiful. I have sharpened her like a sword. I have told her to go and cut off as many heads as she can.' You laughed. 'If she cuts yours off as well, don't blame me.'

I left then and got in my car, told the driver to go as fast as he could. I was banned from driving any of the ranch cars, due to all the minor accidents and unpaid speeding tickets I had, and it rankled me that I had to be driven around like a baby. I never had any choice either about who would drive me. Vishva chose them, and I'm sure she always chose the men who liked me the least. It was never a woman, or anyone from my inner circle.

The driver left the outskirts of the ranch and we made it in record time to the Wasco County council chambers to meet with the politicians.

Those arseholes wanted to ruin me. You know that. They wanted to ruin You as well, but I gladly became their sacrifice. They said we were building illegal housing at the ranch. We were only zoned for forty and already, in our first few months, we had hundreds of sannyasins living there. I told them straight.

'Don't worry about me, if you start demolishing our houses. I will be dead. I will paint your bulldozers with my blood.'

They didn't know what to say so they laughed in an uncomfortable, pained way.

'It's no laughing matter,' I assured them. 'We're trying to build a sustainable commune. We're working together in utter harmony. We're using permaculture principles and growing everything organically. Our animals never get sick. Our fruit trees flourish. Our vegetables have more goodness in them than in all of you stuck together. We're making your Big Muddy Ranch a place the whole world will look at and emulate. And all you're trying to do is stop us.'

I could see them snickering behind their hillbilly hands. Can You see now, Beloved, why I was driven to do the things I did?

Watch out, I thought to myself that day. Watch out or your blood will be painting the bulldozers, not mine.

And yet, it is my blood which paints the walls of this prison cell. I have given up everything for You.

Please write back to me. I deserve, at the very least, an answer.

Ma Anand Sharabo

*

BHAGWAN

AGHIOS NIKOLAOS, CRETE, 1986

I am Zorba the Buddha. I am a meeting of East and West. In fact, I do not divide East and West, higher and lower, man and woman, good and bad, God and devil. I join together all that has been divided up to now.

When I was a boy, I would leave my grandparents' home and stay up all night sitting near the burning ghats on the river. I watched the corpses flaming, moving, shrivelling, becoming fine silky ash as the sun rose. Sometimes they moved, dancing and swaying as if they were still alive. I wasn't afraid. I could recognise something in me that was beyond life or death, past or future.

This body of mine does not belong to me. Whether I abuse it with drugs and alcohol and negativity or whether I honour it with yoga and gratitude and grass-fed cow's ghee makes no difference to me now. I am almost done.

'No, Master,' Vishva murmurs, as she stretches beside me in bed. 'You're too young to leave us.'

Outside, the church bells are clanging. They always clang here, in this odious country. On the hour, every hour. And then whenever there is a service or a saint's day, or a funeral or a wedding, the ear-piercing noise becomes unbearable, lasting longer than any death.

'Yes, Vishva,' I reply. 'Not long to go, now. You will have to learn how to go on without me.'

Her concerned face looms over mine, and she bites her bottom lip in that sad way she has. I rest on my back with my hands clasped on my belly and hardly breathe. It is past noon and we are taking our siesta. Outside, all is still. Not a breath of wind, not a bird stirs. We can just hear the goats, far in the distance on the hillsides. Their bells tinkle like my vanished memories. I have only just woken up and am still half in the world of dreams, and in this state, Vishva's face changes to that of my childhood sweetheart, Shaheena. They are the same person; I know Vishva is her reincarnation.

I draw her down to me and her remote white expression turns into the laughing, broad planes of Shaheena's face. Caramel-coloured limbs, thigh-length hair that falls about her like the clouds of ash from burning corpses.

I have come to Zorba's island to show you how to keep dancing when everything has gone to shit.

*

MUKUNDA

AGHIOS NIKOLAOS, CRETE, 1986

He sits under one of the carob trees in the courtyard and speaks as I imagine Socrates had in my far-off history, in one of my many past lives. His discourses are fiery, more eloquent than any I've heard, even in His Pune heyday. His forthright, honest delivery, His piercing brown eyes. They look into me, through skin and fat and muscle, into throbbing organ and bone. I am burned up. My karma sizzling on the kalpa fire of eternity.

He is aflame. He is speaking to me, but it is more than speech. I feel His words rather than hear them. He is Socrates and I am Plato. I don't need to write this down. It's beyond truth, already hallowed in some ancient record, part of Him and part of me. I can smell the first fragrant carob flowers above my head, heralding spring. I can feel the rough caress of ancient linen robes on my thighs and belly. I feel the knowledge of the ages, the perennial wisdom, welling out of Him like a bubbling spring, like champagne, like His semen, into me.

He is of course critical of Gandhi, Mother Teresa, of Krishnamurti and Ramana Maharshi. He abuses the Pope.

'These people are representatives not of peace but of death. They are liars, they are greedy, they cheat, they abuse. They use nuns as sex slaves. They sexually molest boys and girls. So I say, categorically, that the Antichrist is already in the Vatican.'

He makes fun of the Ayurvedic Indian politicians who drink their own piss. He denounces Greek politicians and the Orthodox Church. I thrill to hear it, having suffered myself as a child and young woman with the chauvinism of Greek men and the narrow-minded judgement of priests and monks.

But I can see some Cretan locals sitting right at the back. Two older men, one younger woman. They don't look happy. Toward the middle of His discourse, they get up slowly, without any overt anger, and walk away. I see Him notice, but he makes no remark on their disappearance. Devamarga sees them out through the wrought-iron gate, with the polite deference he's become so good at.

Shakti leans against me like a child, all hot and dirty, his unwashed hair lank over his shoulders. He's so young, so callow, he can't even grow a beard like the other men. His chin and cheeks are nearly as smooth as mine. His underarms are sparse, reddish with tiny hairs. And he's sweating. Even in the late winter cold, he radiates summer heat. But he's sullen all the time now, since we left London – out of sorts. He isn't listening. He watches Bhagwan's mouth, unmoved. I see Bhagwan glance at him now and then, alert to the unsettling energy he is giving off. I sit up straight and push him off me. I don't want to be contaminated by his lack of conviction. I feel like turning around and slapping his face.

*

SHAKTI

AGHIOS NIKOLAOS, CRETE, 1986

Music plays. Guitars, African drums, tambourines, an Indian sitar, even what Mukunda tells me is the same santouri they used in the Zorba movie. Bhagwan finishes talking and gets up, dances for a few seconds on the porch with Vishva in his shambling, old man's way, and everyone stands up and claps and whoops. I'm bored.

'I teach utter rebellion,' he says before he goes inside, slurring his words. 'Remember this tonight when you walk the streets of the village. Rebellion against anything that does not serve you. Utter rebellion is your birthright.'

How many times have I heard that line before? And what if I want to rebel against him? What if he doesn't serve me?

When he's gone, most of the group heads down to the village to eat and Mukunda and I wander around the villa's gardens, awkward with each other. I know she's angry at me and I have no idea why.

'Do you want to eat something too?' she asks.

I shrug, non-committal.

'Meditate?'

I don't answer.

'Have sex?'

I shake my head.

'What then?' She's using the exasperated tone of voice I've heard so many times before – the school-marm, mother-of-three voice I despise. Just then, I think of my pa and his worn, lined, sunburned face. His big hands, the last hug he ever gave me, leaning over the cow fence at the ranch. I can't think of my ma right now – it's too painful.

'I just wanna go home. I'm sick of all this shit.'

She flinches, and then the steel enters her voice. 'After all this time, if you think what I've shown you here is shit, then there's no hope for you. You're a total waste of my time. All our time. Especially Bhagwan's time.'

It hurts me, what she says, but I square my shoulders and look at her. 'Then I am a waste of time. Get rid of me. Now's your chance.'

She looks incredulous. 'Get rid of you? Take some responsibility, for once in your life. It's what you want, not me. Don't lay it all on me. And don't let me stop you from going.'

'I got no money.'

'I'll take you to the bank tomorrow and give you some. After that, you're on your own.'

She shakes her head and walks off, down the straight double row of olive trees. Her thick, wavy white hair flows down her back, almost reaching her blue-jeaned arse. She doesn't wear red anymore. Her jeans are snug, maybe too tight. I think of her meeting up with one of the sannyasin men down in the village, in a bar; maybe the Swedish or Dutch guys. Real men, not boys like me. I think of her opening her mouth to both of them and trying to peel off her jeans, lying on a bed and getting one of the guys to tug at them. Down to her ankles. Pulling down her underpants. Clamping her hand around their penises, putting her finger in there. The three of them together in bed talking about me, laughing about how immature I am.

Then I realise I really don't care what she does anymore. I don't care about anything. And I don't understand a damned thing.

*

SHARABO

Federal Correction Institution, Dublin, California

February 1986

Bhagwan, my beloved,

I remember walking alongside the Rolls as it billowed down the dirt road in Rajneeshpuram. It must have been soon before I left, sometime in 1984. I am unclear about the time of year; I did that walk so many countless times.

I am at Your side, close enough to touch You, as You sit in the passenger seat and smile and wave. Lining the road are hundreds of our people, waiting to catch a glimpse of You. They throw red roses and pink lilies on the bonnet of the Rolls, until it's heaped with flowers; they soil its creamy whiteness with saffron and cheap powdered incense and their grubby, grasping hands. I am here to shield You from their demands, from their overwhelming love and desire. If I could protect You from the eddies of rising dust I would. If I could stop the sun's rays from hurting Your weak eyes I would do it by burning up my own.

Even though I know of Your numerous and petty betrayals of me, I forgive You. You are old and sick. You have collected around You a shallow and manipulative group of people: Vishva the victim, Devamarga and his new bride Halima, the spoilt bitch from Hollywood, the witch with fake, pumped-up lips. They want to wrest ultimate power from You. That is their plan. I've heard them. That is why I have been forced to wiretap Your bedroom. That is why I have wiretapped the armrest of Your favourite chair. I hear everything. I see everything. I am Your conscience. I am Your holy guardian angel. I am Your inner voice.

I know You want to replace me with Halima. I know You think I am drunk with power, too fierce and self-righteous for my own good. But can't You see that all I do is in Your name?

I have bought You nine hundred cars. I have colluded in Your piss-take of capitalism. I have named the tiny town of Antelope Rajneesh City and called Main Street Mevlana, after one of Your favourite Sufis. I have endured the anger and contempt of the locals for You, so You don't have to suffer. What more can I do?

What more can I do in order for You to recognise who I am?

I will not stop writing these letters. I know in my heart that You read them. I know that You think of me, always. I am a thorn in Your side. I am also the reddest rose: limp, wilted, trampled by hundreds of feet into the dust.

Your servant,

Ma Anand Sharabo

*

BHAGWAN

RAJNEESHPURAM, OREGON, 1984

I have decided to break my four-year silence. Since last night, when Sharabo presided over a meeting and read out passages of a Holy Bible she claimed was the unadulterated Word of Rajneeshism, when I saw the shocked and disappointed faces of my oldest and most loyal sannyasins, I knew I could no longer opt out of this shit show. I can no longer practise silent communication, from my heart to yours. I have decided to speak.

You see, I never wanted to establish a religion. I never wanted to be a guru, or a Moses or Mohammed or a Christ. I am anti-religion. I am anti-guru. I am a buddha, just as you are. We are all buddhas. And just like you, I am also quietly, merely myself. She does not understand this. She never did.

We are alone in my sitting room. Summer is finally here, and the ranch is hot and dry as a Tibetan Buddhist hell. Outside the closed windows, hundreds of flies are buzzing, attracted by the cows and goats and chickens. I feel as if particles of dust have taken up residence in my ears, my throat and nostrils. I can't even generate any sweat. My asthma is coming back, stronger each day, until I feel it choking me like an assassin's hand around my throat.

Sharabo sits opposite, kneeling at my feet, and she is as serene and cool as a glass of water. Fluid and transparent, just like water. I can see right through her now.

She looks up and I see my diminutive self, reflected in her round dark eyes.

'Bhagwan, my beloved,' she says, in a honeyed voice. 'The others are taken ill today.'

I adjust my white silk turban in her mirror-eyes. 'They seemed fine to me early this morning. We all ate breakfast together.'

'They have since developed conjunctivitis. Even Devamarga confirms it. He's checked the others and himself. I've told them they need to leave Lao Tzu before they infect you. If you catch a bug in those weakened eyes of yours, you could go blind.'

'Blind? From conjunctivitis? Surely not. Bring Devamarga to me. What does he say? Bring him here.'

'He's already gone. I don't know where he is right now.'

'What? And the others, where are they? Vishva? Krishna? All of them sick with this thing?'

'Yes, even the cook. We will have to find someone else to prepare your meals. I can do the rest.'

'So, you are my doctor and dentist and companion these days as well as my secretary? Oh, Sharabo, be serious.'

'I am. Those people are infectious. Get rid of them.'

'What do you mean, get rid of them?'

'I merely mean, let them sleep somewhere else for tonight. Tomorrow, if they're better, they can come back.'

'And who decides this? You?'

'Of course not. You do, Bhagwan.'

'Then I will not. I will not get rid of them.'

'You will, because you are a reasonable man.'

'Let me see them.'

'No, they will infect you. Trust me.'

I think then of Zorba's words. 'Everyone follows their own bent,' he said. Sharabo follows her own bent, just as I do. She is like a young tree in the sparse forests that surround us here. She is one type of tree. I am another. We are all trees. Some of us are stunted and battered by heavy winds. Others smooth and upright. Sharabo is a tree, I am a tree. Let her be as she is. Zorba's voice in my head: You've never quarrelled with a fig tree because it doesn't bear cherries, have you?

'I don't trust you,' I say to her. 'Sharabo, I never trusted you. I didn't make you my secretary because I trusted you. I saw you for exactly what you are. And I accepted that. Sometimes I even appreciated it. I thought I could guide you. But now you have become a snake. I never imagined this. Get away from me. Let me speak to my sannyasins now.'

*

MUKUNDA

RAJNEESHPURAM, OREGON, 1984

I have to admit I was a little afraid when they got off the buses. I stood back, wanting to blend into my crowd of fellow sannyasins, not wanting the new arrivals anywhere near me. They were filthy and reeked of ancient sweat and drink and cigarette smoke and the pollution and despair of the cities they had come from.

They were woefully unprepared for early autumn in Oregon, even the ones from nearby Portland. They wore ragged shirts and trousers, no overcoats or scarves. Some didn't even have shoes, or any luggage. I could see Sharabo standing there with her clipboard, taking it all in, keeping tabs on the chaos she had created. We were surrounded by them. Four thousand, she had told us the day before. Four thousand homeless men bussed in from all over the country to vote so we could win our Wasco county election.

I knew it wouldn't end well. I knew on that first night, when the homeless men had been bathed and fed and clothed in our amber and orange and scarlet cast-offs, when they'd been given their extra ration of cigarettes. It was after dinner, when we all had a half-hour to spare before going to bed and getting ready for another early rising. We sat around, drinking herbal teas. The homeless men had been given one bottle of beer each. I had heard some of them demand more, and the way Sharabo shut them down with one of her glares and a few choice words was incredible.

Shakti put an old Rolling Stones record on the player. Jagger belted out I can't get no…I can't get no. The familiar sounds washed over me, and for an instant I felt supremely relaxed, like everything here at the ranch was going to be alright. Shakti stood against the wall, moving his body a little, smoking his last ciga-rette, avoiding me. Or was I being paranoid? Now that he had got used to being at the ranch, made friend-ships, seemed happy, some part of me was afraid that I wasn't enough for him. Too old. Too bossy.

Young girls crowded around him now, asking him to dance. He shook his head, smiling his melancholy, heartbreaking smile. The girls grabbed his arms, managed to twirl him around once, twice. He shook them off and they gave up. They kicked off their shoes and left him, found other men to dance with. They raised their arms in the air, they pirouetted, they shook their hips and laughed. I admired their optimism. Their resilience. They were nothing like me.

It was when two of the homeless men got up too and sidled too close to one of us, a girl in her late teens called Bodha, that I knew things would go horribly wrong. They were young men, no older than thirty, and they already had the dodgy look of long-time criminals. The younger-looking of the two had hardly any teeth left and yet he seemed unashamed, grinning widely.

They started dancing, backing Bodha into a corner, making lewd gestures and bumping their hips against hers, on either side. One of our men stepped in to try and draw her away but they blocked him, silent but solid. I could see Bodha was getting scared. She didn't want to make a scene, didn't want to 'overreact'. I know that face so well, the second-guessing of your own feminine instincts: am I being too sensitive, am I being too precious, it's nothing, don't be a ball-breaker, it's just a bit of fun, they're flirting with you, you should be flattered, get over it. By then, the two men were brushing themselves against her, front and back, with full body contact. They rubbed themselves up against her tight cords, the bra-less breasts they could see under her thin, pink sweater. The other homeless men looked up from their beers and cigarettes, avid now, waiting to see what would happen next. None of our men wanted to step in, fearing a riot and then Sharabo's fierce reaction.

I stood up and turned off the record player. I whipped around and fixed the two men with my best stare.

'Go to bed. Yes, you two, now. Aasar and Shiva will escort you. Bodha, come here. I'll walk you back.'

I stretched out my arm and she took it. Her hand was shaking. I pulled her close to me and held on tight. I looked at the two men again, letting my stern gaze linger over their thin, hounded faces, their blankness, the dead lack of light in their eyes.

'Watch yourselves,' I told them. 'And I'll be watching you too. You don't belong here.'

We lost the election. It was abysmal, even with all the extra votes. The city status of Rajneeshpuram was rescinded and all our subsequent appeals failed. By the end of that year, 2500 homeless men were bussed off the ranch. Only a few of them stayed behind and became sannyasins. Many were unaccounted for: they must have left of their own accord, melted into the mountains or local towns. There were rumours that Sharabo had been mixing sedatives in the beer they were given, which accounts for how compliant they all were after that first night.

I saw those two young men many times since the incident with Bodha, in the kitchens or on the farms. Each time, I stood my ground. They left me alone, and more importantly, left the other, younger, women alone as well. But by December they had vanished. I never saw them board a bus back to where they had come from. Then again, there were so many homeless men sent back or who absconded. I couldn't keep track of them all.

There was a rumour going around after they all left. Some of us claimed that a few of them had died after overdosing on Sharabo's beer and drug combination.

If it was those two harassing Bodha, I was glad. And I'm not ashamed to admit it, even now.

*

SHAKTI

RAJNEESHPURAM, OREGON, 1984

It was late at night, but I wasn't yet asleep when Sharabo shook me by the shoulders. She looked at Mukunda, peacefully asleep on her back beside me, and put her finger to her lips.

When we were outside the huts, she beckoned me to follow her. We scrunched over the greyish powder left from the last snowfall before spring and I watched her slim, red-wrapped body in front of me. Her sannyasin clothes were tight, figure-hugging, custom-made, unlike the other women's. She wore plaited gold leather belts and crazy headdresses, like she was some sort of Egyptian queen. That night, she wore a satiny turban coiled around her head, the colour of wine, and decorated with a pearl necklace adorned with Bhagwan's image. Weird. And expensive. Mukunda had told me all Sharabo's jewellery was the real thing.

I had never been in her private cabin. She wound her way past Lao Tzu House then took me through the stand of firs that marked our northern boundary and down a steep flight of stairs. This couldn't be her cabin. It looked and smelled like a dungeon.

She flicked a switch and in the bright overhead bulb I saw four more faces. They must have looked as stunned as mine. Ashni was there, as well as Padma and Kamini. Sharabo's closest ally, Sadhika, was also there, of course. I'd heard Mukunda call these women the 'temple mums'. They were Sharabo's hench(wo)men. Why was I here with them?

We were sitting in a hired car in The Dalles. Early evening, and a tired drizzle made it hard to see the streetlights or anything else outside the windscreen. Sharabo wasn't there. She had given Padma and me strict, detailed instructions. Ashni and Kamini had already gone in their own hired car to the venues chosen for them in the same city. We were here outside our first designated salad bar restaurant, waiting to go in. Sharabo and Sadhika, the masterminds, stayed back at the ranch. We were on our own now.

Padma was sweating through her heavy clothes.

'Why don't you just take a layer off?' I asked. 'You don't need that big coat.'

She threw me a swift look, like a bird of prey. 'I'm in disguise, idiot.'

I shrugged. I wished I had a Coke, or even some of that kitchari stuff we ate for breakfast that I normally hated. I was starving. Fear does that to me, I think. And I had many fears. The fear that we would be caught. The fear that Sharabo would keep her hands clean and we would be the necessary sacrifices. The dumb ones, the dispensable. The fear that poisoning people was wrong and wasn't worth it anyway. I was committing a mortal sin for nothing. No matter how many people got sick and stayed home and didn't vote, we still wouldn't win the election.

'Your stomach is growling,' Padma said. 'Make it stop.'

I ignored her. I checked my watch – one of Sharabo's. It was nearly time to go in. We both concealed our small plastic jars of salmonella culture under our clothes, the rest in the car. Padma was trembling. When we got out onto the street, I made to take her hand, but she pulled away.

'It'll be okay,' I said.

'Okay? How do you know? We could get life for this!'

It didn't occur to me that anyone could die, could actually shit themselves to death.

*

SHARABO

Federal Correction Institution, Dublin, California

February 1986

Bhagwan, my beloved,

I was so happy at last year's summer festival. I couldn't believe we had managed to acquire twenty thousand sannyasins from all over the world that year. Everyone was dancing and singing. You were glowing. The weather was perfect each day. There were flowers everywhere. So much money was coming in.

I know You cannot forgive me for what I did to Devamarga at the festival. But I swear to You, on my poor mother's and father's lives, that I did it with Your best interests at heart. Devamarga was always aggressive toward me and the other women. He had been for years. He was not speaking to us. He spread rumours about us. He told people he was fully enlightened. How could that be? When You said nobody could attain full enlightenment in this lifetime except You?

I was scared for Your life. I was worried Devamarga and Halima were plotting to assassinate You. I had heard their plans. They wanted to take over the commune and keep the profits for themselves. They were hungry for power. They still are. I get to read the papers in here: all about the people who've left you. The people who hate you. I hear some have committed suicide, others are trying to sue you. Good luck with that!

Injecting Devamarga with adrenaline was not my idea. You must remember that. Sadhika came up with it and carried it out. Of course, I approved it, at the time. I was desperate to save You and had no other options.

Please forgive me. I didn't know what I was doing. All I've ever wanted is for You to be safe.

Your humble servant,

Ma Anand Sharabo

*

BHAGWAN

RAJNEESHPURAM, OREGON, 1985

She is gone. All she left behind is the gold Rolex I gave her back in India, the triple-strand pearl necklaces and silver bracelets, her credit cards, her particular smell. She always smelled of cinnamon gum, though I never saw her chewing it.

I walk through her bedroom, touching her things. It is austere as a monk's cell. There are none of my books, none of my meditation instructions. Not even any photographs or posters of me. The bed is made, aggressively neat. On the wall above it, a generic landscape of a river and weeping willows. There is nothing on the side tables except for a packet of playing cards, well-thumbed, and a lamp shaped like a kundalini snake. She never read spiritual books. She never meditated. She was a ruthless woman. She had no spiritual aspirations. She was utterly materialistic. Yet I admired her practical ways, her feral pragmatism. She was strong-willed, savage. We needed that. The people who are spiritually oriented are star gazers. And I must admit, that is why I made her my secretary. Spiritual people live in the clouds, as I do. We need a good slap sometimes. Sharabo was our metaphorical slap.

She has taken the tapes with her. Now I am scared.

I look everywhere – under the mattress, behind the picture frame on the wall, in the secret safe she told me once she had built into the cupboard. I get down on my hands and knees, groaning, and slide under the bed. Nothing. Not even cobwebs. She was meticulous, thorough. In the ensuite bathroom, another door. I try to open it, but it's locked. She has taken the tapes and she will ruin me.

I step outside her cabin onto the front porch. I raise my arms as high as I can over my head, although it hurts deep in my sinews and bones. Everyone cheers. My sannyasins are dancing among the dust and autumn leaves to celebrate her demise.

I hear she has found sanctuary in West Germany. May the poor Germans rejoice in her.

*

MUKUNDA

AGHIOS NIKOLAOS, CRETE, 1986

I never thought things could get uglier after Sharabo left, but they did. Sitting here under the flowering tamarisk and olive trees, half a world away, it doesn't feel distant at all. It feels too close. Still ugly, and still dangerous.

Sometimes I think the FBI and CIA are still after us. Sometimes I think they can follow us all the way over here and ruin our lives. There is nowhere on this earth safe for Bhagwan. Not even His motherland of India, not Pakistan, not Nepal. He has upset so many people that I fear He will be condemned to wandering the globe until he dies. And what of us?

When we were still at the ranch, we found out Sharabo had poisoned 750 people with salmonella bacteria to prevent them from voting in the county elections. It was called the largest bioterror attack in US history. The FBI found a secret tunnel from Sharabo's bathroom that led to Lao Tzu House. In it were huge caches of firearms, cash and explosives. Bhagwan claimed to know nothing of it. I believe Him, of course.

Devamarga recovered from his attack with the syringe but was ill for many months. He almost died the night of the summer festival. He was in the Portland hospital for three weeks. We realised that the stomach bug we had thought Vishva suffered from that night was also poison. Two Oregonian officials also accused Sharabo of poisoning the water she gave them to drink when they visited the ranch. One thing I'll say about Sharabo: she was indiscriminate in her hatred.

Bhagwan spoke to us that night for the first time in three years. All four thousand of us sat outside, even though the autumn evening was cold. Innumerable stars lit up the night sky, gemmed tears on black eyelashes. Many of us were crying, actually sobbing aloud. To hear Him speak again – to drink in that slow, measured, velvet voice after so long! I closed my eyes and let it fill me up. I let His words permeate every cell and molecule. I was drinking Him in. I felt my hair and skin plumping up as He spoke. I was an opened flower. I was soil after rain. I didn't even care what He was saying.

We circled a bonfire He had made of Sharabo's bibles and all her clothes. I sat toward the front, with only one row of people in front of me. The smell of burning books and cloth reminded me of something I didn't want to face, something distasteful. It felt as if we were placing all the blame of our own mistakes, our blindness, our own out-of-control egos, on one person. It felt too easy. I wanted to move further away. Bhagwan leaned down toward me, as if He sensed the ambivalence I was feeling. He laid his palm lightly on my head for a moment, then bent down and whispered something to Halima. She nodded, turned around and squeezed my hand, once, before facing Him again.

His features were contorted in the red-orange-yellow flames as He spoke. They turned His white hair and beard electric blue and purple. His voice changed now – louder, full of shock and anger.

'Sharabo did not merely use poison,' He began. 'She was poison. Now we purge her from our midst. We forget her, as if she never was. We go back to our roots. We sit, we dance, we work. That is all.'

A few sannyasins got up to twirl around with their arms out wide, half-hearted, but he motioned them to sit down again.

'We will continue to work our land, to make a Paradise out of a desert. We will continue to laugh and love each other. Zorba said that true happiness is to have no ambition and yet to work like a horse as if you had every ambition. This is what we are doing here. We live far from men, as he did, we do not need them and yet we love them. We love them. Yes, we love them! In this vein, I am inviting the FBI to our ashram.

We have nothing to hide. We tell them everything. Enlightenment means I know myself. It does not mean that I know my bedroom is being bugged.'

We laughed, but cautiously, unsure of where His mood would take Him.

'Sharabo has betrayed us,' He continued. 'She has spoken to the FBI herself and given them extensive recordings of our conversations. All of us.' He looked around at our assembled group, many of us shivering in spite of the bonfire. 'She has spoken to the press in Germany.' He held up a pristine, uncrumpled newspaper. In German, the front-page headline read, 'TO HELL WITH YOU, BHAGWAN.'

He threw the paper onto the fire. 'Oh, another thing. It almost slipped my mind. No longer do any of you need to wear red robes or the mala with my image. That time is passed now. You can wear regular clothes, any colour you like. You can put the mala away somewhere safe. Go forward. You need to get on in life. You need to fit in with society if you are to do any good in this lifetime.'

I turned to look at Shakti. He was blank-faced. Devamarga and Halima sat cross-legged in front of me, and even they seemed uneasy at this, raising their eyebrows at each other. It took us all by surprise.

Around me, other sannyasins were shaking their heads, open-mouthed. I could sense my own building elation, but it was still dampened down, a smouldering fire. At the same time, I felt as if a blanket I'd been clutching for years, a soft, warm blanket I'd had since I was a baby, was suddenly ripped away from me and burning on that bonfire.

Vishva, standing tall and slim at Bhagwan's side, seemed unperturbed by His revelation, her face impassive. As we watched, she gently pulled her mala over her head, kissed the image of Bhagwan on it and handed it to Him. With the backdrop of the flames behind her reaching higher and higher, she let her heavy red robe fall to the ground, until it made a sad puddle at her bare feet. Her toenails were expertly manicured. She folded her arms over her belly, like a contemplative Madonna. Close as I was, I could see her skin goose-pimpling at the front and roasting at the back. Her small, high breasts stood out like beacons against her fake-tanned chest and arms and face.

*

SHAKTI

AGHIOS NIKOLAOS, CRETE, 1986

I will never tell Mukunda that I was part of the
bioterror plot. I would rather leave her – as I'm doing
now, leaving this pissy little Greek fishing village for
my real home – than tell her. And maybe that's why I'm
doing it. Maybe that's why I've been so edgy and irri-
table with her since we left Oregon, and those months
in London, since I weaned myself off the hazy oblivion
of drugs and movies and bad daily sex, why I tend to
blame her for every little thing. The guilt of what I did
is eating me.

At the ranch, nobody – not Sharabo in all her press
interviews, or any of the other temple mums who fled
with her – mentioned my name in connection with
the salad bar attacks. And I hope it stays that way. But
I'm still having trouble sleeping at night. I wake in a
cold sweat, here in my starched white single bed, with
the stiff sea breeze rattling the shutters. I wonder if
Bhagwan knows about my involvement. I wonder if he
will look at me one day, open his mouth and destroy
my world. Across the room, I hear Mukunda lying
awake. She coughs, scratches the dry winter skin on
her arms, turns over so she's facing the wall. I open my

eyes and concentrate on the threads of silver moonlight lining the French doors.

But I can't get this one image out of my head: a thin, greenish, viscous film over everything else I see. It's what I imagine salmonella looks like through a microscope. Behind that disgusting little screen, I relive that moment when I upended the contents of the plastic jar over the neat trays of crisp lettuce and cut-up vegetables and dressing, with Padma, my clone, doing the same on the other side.

Thank God they all left. And I don't care anymore if I say God with a big G or a little g or what. Bhagwan can go fuck himself. He thinks he's God. He tells us he's nobody, just a man, just a friend, just a guide – but he thinks he's the centre of the universe. Really. He still goes around saying he knew nothing of any of these plots, that he was an innocent pawn in Sharabo's game. Bullshit. He was the ultimate ringmaster. But how did we, every one of us, fall so completely for him? I don't have a clue. And yet we did. And I did too.

Everyone on the ranch was really scared when Sharabo left. She had given the FBI all the tapes she made of hers and Bhagwan's morning work meetings, not to mention recordings of any private conversation she could get her hands on. I was scared too. What if they mentioned my name in one of their little talks? I was so paralysed with fear I even contemplated asking Bhagwan to protect me. But he was acting insane – or more insane than usual. He was going around accusing Sharabo of poisoning his favourite cow's milk with thallium. He was complaining of hair loss, failing eyesight, weakness in his limbs, ringing in his ears. He stayed in a dark room more of the daytime. When he emerged at night, he yelled at all the sannyasins – including me and Mukunda – who had so readily dropped the red clothes and mala beads. I noticed that Vishva was wearing her robes again, as well as not one but two malas with Bhagwan's image. Doubly proving her devotion.

'Put them back on now,' he told everyone at the next morning discourse. 'It's too early. You're not ready. What? I tell you to do something only last night and straightaway you plunge? Sit on it. Meditate upon it. Contemplate the implications. Understand why you're doing it. Don't be the blind leading the blind. Think for yourselves. And above all, don't wobble.'

The next afternoon, I was taking the cows back to their pens before the sun set. I wore my red-dyed work jeans and faded, pinkish shirt again, and the brown suede cowboy hat I always wore, daring Mukunda or Bhagwan or anyone else to find fault in it. The cows were shifty and mean that afternoon; maybe they were picking up on my mood. Finding them and catching them all took me way further than usual to the outer fence, and I was surprised to see a figure leaning on one of the gates, watching me. My gut lurched. Was he police, FBI? I was too far away to see who it was, whether he was young or old, or whether he was wearing a badge. I thought about turning the other way – cows or no cows – and running. But he would surely have a gun. So I came closer, keeping the bulk of the cows between him and me, until I got near enough to see his face.

He wore a green-plaid shirt and jeans, so it couldn't be a cop, unless undercover. His own cowboy hat was large and battered, shading his face. But when he raised his hand to wave to me, I knew who he was.

When I saw that it was my pa, I guessed straight-away that Sharabo had spilled the beans. My family and I hadn't seen each other or spoken since I joined the ranch. Pa had told everyone in Antelope I was dead to him. My poor ma followed suit, and I know it would have killed her inside to do it.

'Boy, come here.'

I wanted to leap over the gate and fling myself into his arms, but I just stood there, patting one of the cow's flanks, up-down, up-down, watching him through half-closed eyes.

'What do you want, Pa?'

'I need to talk to you. Come here. Look at this.'

He waved the local newspaper at me, and I could just about make out the words: ANOTHER JONESTOWN.

'I'm breaking my silence and anger to save you, boy. Come closer. I won't wallop you.' He chuckled, sourly. 'Not this time, anyways.'

I wanted to say he wouldn't have the balls to wallop me anyways, but instead I came silently to the gate. We were face to face, eye to eye. His eyes were so much like mine: a scoured, shiny green so pale it could hardly be called any colour. I forced myself not to bow my head, fall to my knees, beg his forgiveness.

'You need to leave, Homer,' he whispered. 'This place is too dangerous. You know David Laws, our sheriff? He told me just now, the FBI have that woman Sharabo's tapes. He knows what they all say. Crazy-ass stuff. If the National Guard take the ranch – and we know they're planning to, sooner or later – this charlatan Bhagwan said on the tapes that he plans to form a human shield to protect his sorry carcass. The human shield will consist of the women and children, Homer. You.'

'But I'm a man, Pa, not a kid. He won't use me. They'll give me a gun to protect us with. I won't get shot.'

My pa took me by the shirt collar then and shook me, with a big man's gentleness.

'If the National Guard come in here, Homer, they could shoot you by mistake. Shoot you clean dead. None of us know what could happen.'

I stayed perfectly still, feeling his big, red hands on my shirt collar. How many hundreds of times had he done this to me when I was a kid? I shrugged him off and he released me, already starting to walk away.

'Listen to me for once, son. You're welcome back at home. Tonight. Right now. We forgive you, even though you haven't asked our forgiveness. Your ma says so, and so do I.' He stopped walking, turned around. 'Come with me, now, Homer. You won't have another chance. I won't ask you again.'

*

SHARABO

Federal Correction Institution, Dublin, California

February 1986

Bhagwan, my Beloved,

I have finally attained no-mind. I am living in the pure actuality of this moment. No projection into the future, no nostalgia for the past. I am the impassive witness.

In being this, I release You. I forgive You. You call me Judas to your Jesus. I say there is no me or You, no betrayed or betrayer, no division. You say that You are the one to join together all that has been divided up to now. I say that is my work on this earth too.

I don't care any longer if You read or don't read my words. I know You can feel them. I know they make You shudder and keep You needing me.

Your equal in love,

Ma Anand Sharabo

*

BHAGWAN

RAJNEESHPURAM, OREGON, 1985

The chartered Lear jet waits on the ranch landing strip. I take my time, trying not to show how much I want to leave right now, to run out of this cabin, screaming, not bothering to take anything or anyone with me. But I must not spook my sannyasins. They are counting on me to be calm. I regulate my breathing. I smile. I sit in my favourite armchair and Vishva hands me a Valium and a glass of water.

My chair is coming with me. I watch as Devamarga and Halima load a large, black plastic bag with cash. Is $174,000 enough for now, Bhagwan? They throw in thirty-five gold, sapphire and emerald watches – we can sell them if we need to – and a .38 handgun loaded with Teflon bullets, to penetrate bulletproof vests. When will we ever need to use this? They all seem uncomfortable with the firearm, but I tell them I do know how to fire a gun. Vishva clutches all our passports in her freshly manicured hands. When, in Shiva's name, did she have time for a manicure?

The Fed informer told us early this morning that I will be arrested without bail within forty-eight hours. We didn't know whether to trust him and had no idea what he hoped to gain by telling us. Maybe he was just a blabbermouth. Maybe he was playing a double game and hoping to be paid twice. We gave him some money – not too much – and he took it. We hope he won't be back.

It's two in the afternoon now and the pilot is becoming restive. He doesn't want to be involved in a gunfight, in case the National Guard come storming in soon. He thinks we are leaving so suddenly because I am sick and need urgent medical treatment. At least, that is what he likes to think. But he knows the story beneath the story. We all do.

Halima and Devamarga are flapping about, picking up first one thing, then another, cramming what they can find into the plastic bag. It's so heavy it looks like it will split as soon as they pick it up.

'Leave everything else,' I command. 'The others can mail the things we need, wherever we end up.'

It is the first time in my life I am leaving a place with no idea where I need to go next. My days on this earth are numbered. I am finished.

*

MUKUNDA

RAJNEESHPURAM, OREGON 1985

I'm surprised Bhagwan looks so healthy here in Greece, considering how bad He was when He left Oregon. At the ranch, we all came to the landing strip to watch Him take off. There weren't many of us left on the land by that stage – maybe a third of what we had been even a few weeks ago. So many left when they caught wind of the FBI involvement and the threat of the National Guard. They flew home to the UK and France and Australia and Japan while they still could. They tried to flee the oncoming storm.

Not me or Shakti. We stood there, hands clasped together, as Bhagwan passed us with His slow, shuffling gait, leaning heavily on Vishva. His hands were shaking. It was hard to believe He was only in His fifties. He mounted the steps to the Lear jet with difficulty and turned at the top to bow His head and bring His arms out wide, blessing us. He wore large, dark, square-framed sunglasses and the wind whipped at the silver and white bell-shaped sleeves of His robe. It raised dust devils around us, obscuring my last glimpse of Him as He entered the plane. At that point, everything slowed down. Rajneeshpuram, the city that would never die, was playing out its last gasps. It had ended. We were done.

When we heard that Bhagwan had been apprehended at Caroline airport, we didn't know whether to stay or go. By then, there was a mere handful of us remaining at the ranch. Discipline was lax and sustained work was non-existent. We had no leaders. We had no idea if we would all have to flee the next day. But we kept hanging on, hoping Bhagwan would send us a sign.

Thank goodness for Shakti and some of the other farm boys, otherwise we would have starved. On those cold, late autumn nights, we ate our meagre portions of plain brown rice and sweet potatoes, sitting huddled around one tiny TV screen in the dining hall. When we saw Our Master being led away from that airport with shackles on his wrists and ankles, flanked by armed guards, we fell apart.

I remember convulsing and sobbing, not being able to stop. Instinctively, I mouthed the prayer I recalled from my childhood Orthodox church-going days: Kyrie isou Christe, ie tou Theou, eleison mas, amartoli. Lord Christ, Son of God, have mercy on us, sinners. Eleison. Mercy. In the midst of my panic, I was angry and disgusted with myself. In crisis, I couldn't believe that I would revert to the old myths. I had no hope of enlightenment. But I couldn't get that phrase out of my head. Kyrie eleison. Eleison. From olive, the sacred green oil of forgiveness. Have mercy on us. Bhagwan, anoint us with Your grace. I remember Shakti's skinny, hairless arms around my shoulders, the way he tried to comfort me like a grown man. I remember muttering that Greek Orthodox phrase under my breath, against my will, over and over. It was lodged in my brain. I remember not being able to eat or walk or drink, feeling disembodied for days, and still that phrase continued inside me, waking or sleeping. Kyrie eleison.

We had no idea where Bhagwan was after they arrested Him. He had been taken from one prison to another every two to three days. It had been twelve days so far. In Oklahoma, He was mistreated and put to sleep on a mattress that He insisted was impregnated with thallium by the CIA. Thallium. He seemed to think it was at the root of all his ills.

The last evening at the ranch before we left for London, we watched Bhagwan's interview with Ted Koppel on Nightline. Our Master looked hounded, guilty. We didn't want the world to see Him like that.

His eyes were glazed, bloodshot. His irises pinned, like a drug addict, and shiny with unshed tears.

Koppel was brutal. He called Rajneeshpuram 'Rancho Rajneesh', as if we were in some bad Western movie. He spoke over Bhagwan. He raised his voice. He interrupted and rolled his eyes.

'I cannot go to jail,' Bhagwan insisted, over and over. 'Because I have done nothing wrong. They have made the innocent a criminal. Democracy is all hocuspocus. It is simply hypocrisy.'

Koppel ignored Him. 'I can't believe why people should go on giving you watches to wear and Rolls Royces to drive. And not one but ninety-three Rolls Royces and hundreds of watches.'

Bhagwan raised His arm casually so that His sleeve fell away and exposed the watch He wore. It was the gold one with the seven sapphires.

'Ted, you do not know the ways of pure love.'

'But I have close friends, Bhagwan. Plenty of them.'

'A friend is one thing. But you do not have a Master. You have never loved anybody more than you love yourself. The moment you love somebody more than yourself, then you are ready to do anything for that person.'

'I love my Jesus.'

'Do you, really? Do you love this Jesus of yours? Would you be willing to give up your life for him? My sannyasins would do that for me.'

Koppel looked foolish, studied his sheaf of notes. At that moment Bhagwan looked straight at the camera: pure, unblinking. In that look I saw my past, my present and my future. I saw the crackling energy of the galaxies, the bold sweep of the universe. We got up off that cold concrete floor and danced around, clapping and yelling and cheering for Our Master. The Orthodox phrase continued in my head, eleison, eleison, eleison, unchecked, a counterpoint to our raised voices and outstretched arms.

*

SHAKTI

AGHIOS NIKOLAOS, CRETE, 1986

She drove me to Heraklion airport in one of Bhagwan's cars, given to him by a Cretan sannyasin. It wasn't a Rolls this time. It wasn't even a new car. It was dirty, beaten up. It smelled of sweat and cigarette smoke. The whole drive, she was silent and kept her face averted from me. On her sunken cheeks, the tracks of all the tears she'd shed last night. I tried to speak to her, but she wasn't listening. Anyway, it was hard for me to explain why I had to leave. I didn't fully understand it myself.

Last night, I'd been commanded to see Bhagwan for my first and final darshan. Maybe Mukunda had asked him, maybe she thought it would make me stay. Maybe he came up with it himself. Anyway. I knelt in front of his scrubbed, pink feet and closed my eyes. He leaned forward from his chair and placed his thumb and fingers in the middle of my forehead. As soon as he touched me, I felt a jolt of electricity run down my spine. It was so real it hurt. Behind my closed eyes, his white-bearded face formed and unformed and his eyes blazed like torches.

'I don't teach the Middle Way, Shakti,' he pronounced, in that slow-motion, underwater way he had. 'I teach the Total Way. In me you will find it – but perhaps not yet.'

As soon as he spoke, the intense images and sensations vanished. I had trouble, even a second later, remembering how overwhelming it had been.

'Open your eyes.' He leaned back again and surveyed me.

'You, Shakti, are only just beginning. You are still a foetus. You have many lives – countless lives – ahead of you. You will remember me in one of those lives, you will find the Total Way, but not for many thousands of years.'

What the fuck did that mean? I left his sitting room in a fog of disbelief. And anger. Yeah, there was that. I was angry he didn't recognise all I'd done for him in this life. I'd given up so much for nothing.

Mukunda parked the car in a No Standing zone and we got out. Three chain-smoking policemen walked up to us and told her she couldn't park there. She yelled at them in Greek and English and started throwing her money around. They yelled back. Soon, they accepted her money and even carried my bag to the terminal, offering me a cigarette when we arrived.

My flight was delayed. Mukunda and I sat outside, watching people get out of cars and tractors and trucks, loaded down with huge black and white chequered plastic bags, cardboard boxes tied with rope and crates of chickens and geese. The sun was fierce, even for an early spring morning. Summer's heat was only a moment away.

A stray kitten leaped up on the bench between us, purring and rubbing herself on my thighs. I put out my hand to pat her.

'Don't touch it,' Mukunda said. 'They're all sick, these strays. They could give you ringworm, or worse. Psst!' she said to the cat, flapping her hands. 'Fighe. Go away.'

I kept patting the kitten in slow, long strokes down her flanks. 'It's okay. I don't care what she gives me. I'll deal with it. She's just so cute.'

The kitten continued purring, writhing in ecstasy as I rubbed her tummy. Then she bared her little claws and tried to give me play-bites.

'Yuck,' Mukunda kept saying. 'Saliva's all over you. It's diseased. How can you be so stupid?' And then she began to cry. 'You're so stupid, Shakti,' she kept saying. 'I gave you everything and you're just throwing it away to go back to your old life. Your old life of such dark-ness, such ignorance and stupidity.'

I couldn't take it anymore. 'Don't call me Shakti again, okay? That's not my name. And it's your own fucking stupidity we should be talking about. I'm only nineteen, for God's sake. You made me get the snip, when I didn't know any better. When I was so in love with you, I would have done anything you asked. You used me so badly, and so did your idiot guru Bhagwan.'

She tried to touch me then, on the arm, but I jerked my whole body away from her.

'I hate you,' I said. 'I hate the person I've become with you. And I hate him even more.'

When I needed to board, she came with me past baggage control. Nobody stopped her. She held on to me so tight I thought she was going to break my ribs. I buried my face in her soft, white, jasmine-smelling hair and let myself slump into her body. She was thin, sharp-angled, like an old lady. It was then I felt a lurch of disgust, keener than any time before.

When I pulled away, her face was wet with tears. She looked like death. Her death, and mine.

'Goodbye, Kalliope,' I said.

She opened her mouth to say something, then closed it abruptly. I turned around and walked onto the tarmac. It felt so good to say goodbye, to put her behind me. To forget I'd ever been that person. It felt so good to finally let go.

*

SHARABO

Federal Correction Institution, Dublin, California

February 1986

Bhagwan, my Beloved,

If You don't reply to me, just once, I will bring You down. I promise You. You, of all people, know I can.

Your Nemesis,

Ma Anand Sharabo

*

BHAGWAN

AGHIOS NIKOLAOS, CRETE, 1986

This fat, stupid Bishop Dimitrios has it in for me. It doesn't matter to him how many sannyasins have come to Crete to boost the economy in the low season, to pay for rooms and food and alcohol and souvenirs.

It doesn't matter to him that I preach peace and love, which he should be doing, instead of spewing his hatred and bile. He doesn't care that the previous Prime Minister, Georgios Papandreou, personally signed a month-long visa for me.

This bishop has been sending telegrams to the new PM and the President and all the Greek newspapers. He is threatening to dynamite Villa Galini if I don't leave. Very Christian. His latest telegram was breathtaking in its stupidity. 'Either he stops preaching or we use violence. Blood will flow should Bhagwan not leave the island voluntarily.'

The reason he gives is laughable. 'Corrupting the youth', just like Socrates. Of course I am corrupting his youth! These hollow-headed, dull, pious Greek children need corrupting. They need the scales ripped from their eyes. Saint Paul didn't know what he was talking about. There is a whole new world out there. And here they are, these blinded children, running to confess their sins to black-robed priests and waiting until they're married in a church to have boring, blinds-drawn sex with the spouse their parents and grandparents have chosen for them. They need some corruption. They need to get some new ideas in their heads.

I have been writing my own letters to the Greek press. They can look in the mirror and see the foolishness of this culture they have created, with their piss-weak Christianity and sexism and racism and parochialism. Let them drown in their isms. Let them flail around in their made-up sins. They have created this warped morality in two thousand years, and if this morality and religion which has been created in two thousand years can be destroyed by a mere tourist like me in four weeks, then it is well worth destroying.

*

MUKUNDA

AGHIOS NIKOLAOS, CRETE, 1986

Bhagwan has asked us to talk some sense into the Bishop of Crete. He knows it's the only way he can stay on the island, but it's the very last thing I want to do. Those religious men give me hives. And since Shakti left, I haven't felt like doing anything. The high elation I felt at being here with my Master has faded to dishwater grey. I mope around the villa's gardens. I can hardly eat. I read whichever paperbacks are on the villa's shelves. Dante. Robert Graves. The King James Bible. A copy of Zorba the Greek. I sleep a lot. Or, I'm in bed a lot, trying to sleep.

I write Eleni a brief note. In it, I decide not to betray how exhausted, how unstable, how sick of life I am. Instead, I urge her to forget our differences and come to Crete to see me. You don't have to see the Master, I write. You and I can go stay in a nice hotel. I love you, my darling child. I miss you. Please come. I get no reply.

I take Ma Amira with me to see the bishop. Her husband, Thanassi, is Greek, and I figure I need some support from someone who understands. Someone who understands the strange pull of guilt and sorrow and fascination I have with my background. Someone who can pretend to understand, even if she really has no idea.

We put on our most modest clothes, large buttoned shirts and long skirts – why the hell do we have to, I hear you ask, and I wonder the same thing – and we even wear black scarves over our tied-back hair. Now we look like right old Greek grandmothers.

The church and monastery aren't really that far from the villa, so we walk. We figure it's more humbling to walk anyway. Amira even brings a posy of flowers she gathered from the villa gardens. Not much is growing yet, so the posy is mostly wilting carob blossoms and sticks and green leaves.

We trudge up a steep hill and by the time we get there, we're sweating through our heavy clothes and scarves. I take mine off to flap at my hair a bit, just to cool the nape of my neck. Amira raises her skirt to get some air underneath. Just as we stop and do so, an old woman emerges from the church door.

'Hairete. We're here to see Bishop Dimitrios,' I call out in Greek, nodding to her formally.

Amira lets her skirt fall and smiles, raising her hand in greeting.

The old woman stares so hard I think she's trying to hypnotise us. She spits on the ground and makes the sign of the evil eye, not once but three times. 'You!' she shouts. 'You are the devil's daughters. You dare come to the monastery? Get out of here!'

We cautiously come closer. 'We only want to see the bishop. Is he here? We have something important to tell him, from our master.'

Amira holds out the flowers, and the old woman knocks them to the ground. They scatter over the front steps, ruined.

'Out of my sight, whores! Now! Don't you dare desecrate God's house with your evil ways.'

The bishop comes to the high doorway with a scrunched-up face.

'What is going on here, Marika? Why do I hear such words?'

When he sees us, he draws himself up to his full height.

'Out!' he bellows. 'Out of my sight, serpents! Get out before I kill you!'

We both recoil. I remember that scene in the film version of Zorba the Greek, where the village widow, played by Irine Papas, is beaten, stoned and stabbed to death by her fellow villagers after they find out she had slept one night with the foreigner. I am filled with an illogical, unnameable dread.

'But, please, if you would just listen –' Amira begins in her terrible Greek, and the old woman makes as if to push her backward. I grab her by the arm as she stumbles against me in surprise.

'No use,' I whisper to her, and we both turn and walk away.

I am so angry at myself for feeling scared. My legs are trembling so hard, I just want to run. But they're watching us, standing there on the church steps, arms folded over their black-clothed bellies, and the last thing I want is for them to see my fear.

*

SHAKTI

ANTELOPE, OREGON, 1986

None of the locals talk to me anymore. I don't look any different. I dress in plaid shirts and jeans. I've shaved my beard off and cut my hair. I don't sound any different. I make sure to talk slow, not the rapid-fire, clipped Queen's English that was Mukunda's way of speaking. But I am different. I know it, and they know it. I just don't know how to go back to who I was.

My ma doesn't know what to say to me. She sits on the rocking chair and looks at me, wrings her hands without knowing she's doing it, and the tears course down her cheeks. She's so unaware of them she doesn't even bother wiping them away. I lean over and do it for her, with the hem of my shirt.

'I used to feed you your evening bottle in this here chair, Homer, when you were a baby,' she says.

I nod, and she can't think of anything else to say, so we revert back to our customary silence.

We sit in the back screened porch, watching the day die. The sun sets in a pomp of glory out west, and for a few moments it stains us with red and orange and bright yellow and pink. His colours. The colours of dirt and dust and blood. The colours of the ranch. Even my ma, washed by those shades, is infected by him. I want to punch his face. I want to protect her from his influence, from the way he's turned her life and all our lives to hell. I want to kill him for ever being born.

I couldn't get a job anywhere for months when I got back from Greece. And I tried. Only yesterday morning, I went to the local canning factory and applied. Nothing. Even though they'd put an ad in the paper saying they were desperate for workers. I knew what I had to do. I'd been avoiding it, but I knew it was inevitable. I went to the slaughterhouse yesterday afternoon. Surely, they'd need me there. And they did.

So here I am today, just home from my first day at work. I'm too tired to wash my hands or have a shower or change my clothes. I must reek but I can't smell it anymore. My ma wrinkled her nose, but she still hugged me when I got home. Now she kneels at my feet to pull off my work boots. Seeing her bowed grey head beneath me, the way she struggles, the cracked leather filthy with blood and hair and entrails, I start shaking.

'No, Ma, I can do it.' I lean down, fumbling at my laces.

It reminds me too much of him and his followers. The kneeling, the bowing at his feet. I feel like vomiting.

I fling my boots into the corner and proceed to fall apart. I'm shaking and crying. I'm howling like a wolf. I can't breathe. She stands in front of me and brings my head down to rest against her belly. Her house dress smells like cut-up onions and dirt and perfumed talc. Her hands on the back of my shorn head are rough and soft at the same time. We stay like that, me shaking and crying, her holding my head hard against her, until it's dark.

When my pa comes home, we pretend nothing ever happened.

*

SHARABO

Federal Correction Institution, Dublin, California

March 1986

I have decided not to betray You. You deserve it, for spurning me so resolutely. But I am better than You. If I betrayed You, I wouldn't be able to live with myself. And I hate to think how many more lifetimes I would have to endure to atone for it.

For You, I have stood trial for attempted murder. For You, I have been convicted and sentenced to three terms of twenty years.

Bhagwan, I can't help it.

I will always love You.

*

BHAGWAN

AGHIOS NIKOLAOS, CRETE, 1986

I crawl with great effort out of my nightmares into an early afternoon speckled with light, like the underside of a hen's egg. The pale green shutters are drawn against a bitter wind. The low ceiling, the white walls, the smooth stone floor, washed with bright coins of sunlight. God changes his appearance every second. Blessed is the man who can recognise him in all his disguises. I see God in the sunlight. I see God in the flat stones. I see God in the wash of reflected ocean blue across the sheets. But I cannot see God in myself any longer. Oh, Zorba. I can't live up to your bliss and joy and daring.

Vishva, beside me, is still asleep. Her face is freckled with gold and silver. It's rare I get to see her face unguarded. Usually she is so composed, like an idealised marble statue of herself. A Greek goddess. I turn to one side, careful of my aching back, and watch her chest rising and falling, the slightest movement, her small nostrils flaring with each breath. She breathes. She is alive.

I, on the other hand, am already dead. I raise my right hand in front of my face and study it, taking in the enlarged veins and knuckles and joints, the mottled age spots, like a toad. How could this have happened to me? To me, of all people? Vishva opens her eyes. I close mine again and whisper into her ear.

'Vishva, listen to me. Vishva. Heed my words. Death makes fools of us all. But if everything goes according to me, every one of us will die as Zorba the Buddha. Between the Greek and the Buddha there is not much distance, but first you must be the Greek.'

I can see that she does not understand. She stares into my face, reading the vertical lines of age on my cheeks, the furrow of worry between my brows. 'How do we become Greek, Master? I thought you hated the Greeks.'

I ignore her. I can hear something going on downstairs.

There is a sound like a brick hitting the window directly below us. Raised Greek voices. The voice of my lawyer, Omkar, yelling in protest. A loud slap. I sit up. My back goes into spasm, with a black pain so vivid it is more like ecstasy. I scream. Vishva puts her hand on my chest, gently lowers me down.

'Stay here, Master. Try to rest. I'll go and look.'

She puts on her red bathrobe with trembling hands, runs out the bedroom door, closing it firmly behind her. I lay there for a minute, listening. When I think my back will allow me, I slowly sit up and get out of bed, leaning on my cane. Before I can make it to the door, I hear thudding footsteps coming up the stairs. Many feet. Booted feet. My bedroom door is being kicked in.

'No,' I can hear someone say. 'Ochi! Leave him alone. I'm pleading with you.' Mukunda bursts in with seven Greek policemen jostling her, guns at the ready.

'Sir, you come with us,' one of them says in thick, broken English. 'You come to Heraklion, now.'

Mukunda turns on him and snarls.

'Don't you touch him!' she says in English. 'Don't go near him!' Then a stream of curses in Greek.

'Mukunda.' My voice is still cracked from sleep. My eyes strain at the brightness. 'No need. Do not worry. These are donkeys, they do not understand.'

She is wild, her white hair flying. One of the policemen tries to restrain her arms from behind and she headbutts him in the jaw.

'Mukunda!' I step forward. 'We want no trouble.'

The policeman she hurt pushes her down onto the bed on all fours. He holds her head down onto the mattress, twisting her neck cruelly. His thick fingers sink into her flesh. I too sink down, next to her. I catch his eye, raise both my palms, open, to him. He releases her and I draw her to me, holding her face against my chest. She is dripping with snot and tears, sobbing, finding it hard to draw breath. There are livid marks on her neck and upper arms.

I can hear more of them downstairs, overturning furniture and vases, looking in toilets and under rugs and in bathroom cabinets. Vishva's high-pitched voice, pleading with them not to disturb me. They are looking for drugs and cash and who knows what else? They will not find anything.

Upstairs they rip open the shutters until my bedroom is swimming in light. The wind whips through the windows, setting papers and sheets and clothes flying. They tear down the curtains, pull everything they can find out of drawers and cupboards, make us stand against the wall so they can strip the bed. I look at Mukunda, hoping to make her feel some of my own hard-won calm and acceptance. Her face is a tight, painful, red ball. I reach out and take her small, sweating hand in mine.

Outside, I hear the church bells clanging again, but this time they do not stop. They are calling to me, hammering in my brain, forcing me to go. They are celebrating my death. They ring out beyond the fields and hillsides, into the village and over the harbour. They continue across the entire island, from churches to monasteries to mountain chapels. The policemen hear them too and make the Orthodox sign of the cross – an ancient flurry of hands, like a choreographed folk dance.

'Do not fight them,' I mouth to Mukunda. 'Do not incite them to more violence.'

She nods. A last single tear rolls from the corner of her eye down her cheek. I put out my finger to catch it.

Forgive them. They know not what they do.

Never born, never died, visited this planet between December 12, 1931, and January 19, 1990.

Bhagwan's self-written epitaph

When shall I at last retire into solitude alone, without companions, without joy and without sorrow, with only the sacred certainty that all is a dream? When, in my rags — without desires — shall I retire contented into the mountains? When, seeing that my body is merely sickness and crime, age and death, shall I — free, fearless and blissful — retire to the forest? When? When, oh when?

Zorba the Greek, Nikos Kazantzakis

Essay

I didn't know anything about him, except that his followers wore shades of red and in the early '80s the media called them 'Rajneeshis', or 'Orange People.' There were money laundering scandals, international court cases, attempted murder, prison sentences and a memorable Australian Sixty Minutes TV interview where his personal assistant and spokesperson, Ma Anand Sheela, shot back 'tough titties' at journalist Ian Leslie when he dared question her on the finances of the spiritual movement.

We all thought they were a cult. They were scary – kidnapped people, took their money and wouldn't let them leave. I grew up Greek Orthodox: Sunday School every week, Byzantine icons in every room, the oil lamp and frankincense lit before church. Gurus were anathema. According to my mother, non-Christians wouldn't necessarily go to hell – not knowing any better – but we couldn't be sure. Even non-Orthodox Christian denominations were not immune to hellfire. So, to renounce everything and follow a guru was unthinkable.

And Bhagwan Shree Rajneesh, or Osho, as he later called himself, was a guru like no other. He was called 'the most dangerous man since Jesus Christ' – confronting, provocative, outrageous, even offensive. He trampled on sacred cows. He made fun of bishops, monks and priests of all religions. Notoriously, he called Mother Teresa a charlatan and hypocrite and Mahatma Gandhi a mere businessman. He called Pope John Paul II the antichrist. He made fun of fundamentalist Hindus who drank their own urine and famously said, 'Esoteric means bullshit.' He was the anti-establishment leader of a rebellion unlike any other.

His hundreds of thousands of disciples – sanyassins – wore saffron, scarlet and rose-coloured robes and jeans, long, wild hair and beards, and 108-bead malas around their necks with his image on them. They came to him from all over the world. They danced, screamed, kicked, jumped up and down like Masai warriors, drank alcohol, took drugs and made love to multiple partners with abandon. They met on Indian beaches at sunrise for Dynamic Meditation. They practiced another three-hour a day, three-week meditation called Mystic Rose, which involved laughing, sobbing, then complete silent witnessing. Their guru preached radical self-acceptance.

Sanyassin, in Sanskrit, is directly translated as 'lay it down.' A sanyassin is one who has given up everything – money, family, education, culture, status – to follow the guru. It is an ongoing process of renunciation and unravelling. To be a sanyassin is to recognise the light of the divine in the guru, to see the guru as a mirror of your own enlightenment. He reflects back to you all that you are. Osho was a light-hearted rascal guru, a self-confessed 'spiritual playboy' and 'crazy wisdom' master. He made jokes. He drank wine, ate whatever he liked and had sex with his followers. He enjoyed jacuzzis. He swore. His slow-motion discourse on the many permutations of the word 'fuck' has been watched by thousands on YouTube. He said, 'Once you get a big enough bite of that great cosmic orgasm, you realise that sex is not the only way to have bliss.' At the same time, there was a lot of sex also going on in his Pune ashram and his ill-fated Oregon ranch, Rajneeshpuram.

Yet beneath the false construct of his ego trappings, his wealth, status and power, the gold Rolex watches and ninety-three Rolls Royces, Osho's tantric teachings were real. Love yourself, even the worst bits. Celebrate life in every single moment. Embrace sensuality. Don't deny the needs and desires of your body. Respect it and work with it consciously. Integrate all dimensions of the body, mind and spirit to 'become the whole.' Osho was only interested in utter inner transformation, nothing less – transcending the personal and integrating both the darkness and the light.

He urged his followers not to worry about Nirvana or awakening. Every moment was a new opportunity to unfold – yes, like a big, red-hearted mystic rose. There was no ultimate goal. 'Life is not a problem to be solved,' he said. 'Only a mystery to be lived.' Awakening – or enlightenment as he preferred to call it – could be an obstacle, if it's the only thing you focus on, if you're fixated on that ladder climbing ever upward to the last stage. There is no last stage and the striving is merely another attachment to discard. Enlightenment is your nature, he said, in one of his thousands of discourses. You are already there. 'To be natural is to be enlightened. A state of being natural… is not an achievement…it is available, relax into it. The deeper you go, the more you find yourself empty.' You are pure, universal consciousness without doing a single thing.

I didn't know any of this when my family and I moved from Sydney to northern NSW in late 2017, to a home high on a ridge overlooking national park, the Pacific Ocean and Byron Bay's lighthouse. When our landlord told me there was an ashram across the road, I made a mental note to avoid it. Something in me was both fearful and dismissive. I still clung onto the residue of my own fundamentalist upbringing. But as time went on, I got to know the people who lived and worked there. They were just like me. They grew vegetables, painted pictures, practised yoga and had regular Wednesday night vegetarian dinners where everyone was welcome. It gave me an insight into the mundane ordinariness, if you like, of the life of people who once followed a guru's every word, who once committed what would be considered by some to be subversive acts. Their lives and the issues they struggled with were much like mine. We had more similarities than differences. They had bought the forty-hectare acreage in the '80s when land was cheap in the shire and created a wildlife corridor and koala sanctuary, an eco-conscious, intentional community and a living shrine to their guru.

After the spectacular collapse of Osho's 1981-1985 Oregon experiment, Rajneeshpuram, documented in the recent Netflix documentary Wild, Wild Country, many sanyassins went home. A core group followed him into exile in 1986 as he circumnavigated the globe, stopping in 21 countries to look for sanctuary and finally ending up again in Pune, India. Most scattered. Many left the teachings altogether, feeling they had been irreversibly tainted by Osho's arrest under the Reagan government, the involvement of the FBI, the CIA and INTERPOL, and his personal assistant Sheela's indictment for attempted murder. Here in Byron, the group still practiced daily 6am Dynamic Meditation. But Gondwana, as the property is called, was less like a hippie commune than a loose community of like-minded people with their own well-appointed homes and jobs and busy lives.

Rajneeshpuram was a 26,000-hectare ranch in Oregon, a 'buddha field' with its own hospital, school, post office, organic farms and airport, which chewed up US$125 million of sanyassin money. Before its collapse, the media was calling it another Jonestown. Osho (or Sheela, depending whose narrative you believe,) had stockpiled guns, bombs and chemicals for biological warfare. Under Sheela's command, her inner circle of so-called 'temple mums' attempted to kill Osho's personal physician, conducted illegal wiretapping and poisoned over 700 people in the city of The Dalles by infecting two salad bars. The commune established a 'Peace Force' instead of a police force, trained by the local militia. Sheela was saying, 'I don't believe in Jesus' way of turning the other cheek. I go for both cheeks.' Later, Osho insisted that Sheela had been defying him all along, as he had been in silence for 3.5 years and knew nothing of her plans.

Yet Osho always urged his followers not to believe anything he said, and you could claim Sheela was following this particular precept fully. His biggest fear was that after he died his disciples would create a static, calcified religion out of his teachings. Sheela went one step further and published a bible, an actual holy book of his teachings, and called him the head of the church of 'Rajneeshism.' But Osho wanted no church and no holy book. 'The happy person needs no religion,' he said. 'The happy person needs no church or temple, because the whole universe is a temple.' He was against all 'isms' and this is partly why he cultivated such an unpredictable persona, changed tack all the time, contradicting himself daily. 'I want to destroy all belief systems,' he said. 'I have been constantly inconsistent so that you will never be able to make a dogma out of me. You will simply go nuts if you try.' This is in stark contrast to most, if not all religions and spiritual teachings – the 'dead traditions', except for some forms of Buddhism such as Zen.

This is what drew me to Osho and fascinated me enough to write some version of his story. In 2018, when I lived opposite Gondwana, I spent much of that year researching. At first, I was convinced Osho was a con man and a liar. As the year progressed and I tried some of his techniques, spoke to people, read piles of books, I understood his appeal. I finally came to the realisation that he intimately understood human nature. That my own never-ending, cyclic path to integration is not unique, and moreover, is exactly the way it should be. That my pettiness, frustration, jealousy and rage is shared by every human, and may in fact be the actual path. The obstacle is the path. We're so used to attaining, working at something, perfecting it, being 'good.' Osho's teachings made me realise there is another way. What if letting your shoulders drop, closing your eyes, just relaxing, is the way to go? This realisation goes hand in hand with an understanding of our interconnectedness, and only then can we approach the idea of compassion, of self and selflessness, of no separation between ourselves and the rest of the world.

Osho recognised the neurotic Western mind. He acknowledged our restless, speedy seeking. Our lack of self-worth. Our wide-ranging discontent, our need to always achieve. His first premise was that we are all mad to varying degrees. Mad souls in a sick society, trying to survive. 'Meditation is medicinal,' he said. 'Only if you are ill, is it needed.' His goal was for his disciples to go beyond identities: race, religion, gender, sexuality, age, profession, ethnicity, culture. He understood that the goal of dominant Western culture is always to be something, yet Eastern spirituality embraces the concept of being no thing. Nothing. Starting with nothing, ground zero, to find our centre. Stopping the thinking, planning, worrying, obsessing.

He saw the unbalanced nature of our desires, the unnatural way of life we think is the norm. 'We're all a bundle of neuroses', he said. Traditional Eastern methods of breath and sitting meditation didn't work so well for Westerners. He recognised our need for methods of physical and emotional release because we've become so contracted, guilty, repressed and depressed. Osho's trademark meditations were preparatory, purging, fiery practices. They pushed you into a heightened state of self-observation. I've tried Dynamic Meditation a number of times. It is a five-step process which involves deep, fast breathing through the nose; full body release which can involve crying, screaming, hitting objects, kicking and throwing yourself around; jumping up and down with your arms up over your head chanting the mantra 'Hoo!'; standing in stillness and silence then lyrical, free dance. It's a true workout, a catharsis and cleansing, and even though I regularly sprint, swim, garden and lift weights, I didn't have the physical or emotional stamina for a whole uninterrupted hour. I needed many breaks. My legs and arms were jelly. By the end, I was sweating from every pore and short of breath. Osho said, 'You open an abyss before them and tempt them to jump.' And that's exactly what it felt like.

In Crete in 1986, where Osho spent a mere two weeks before being deported, his health, which had never been robust, began to fail further. This period is the focus of my novella, the brief hiatus he experienced in a clifftop villa by the sea, before the Greek authorities threw him out of their country. Here, the disc pain in his lower back intensified, his heart rate was erratic, he had diabetes and a possible nitrous oxide (laughing gas) addiction. He could do no more than shuffle from bed to bathroom to a cushioned seat under the olive trees for his disciples' daily darshan (from the Sanskrit darsana which means 'seeing' of the divine, or 'to be in the light of the master'). He was only in his mid-fifties. Later on, he believed that he had been poisoned with radioactive thallium by the CIA and the Reagan government, when he was shunted from prison to prison in the US after the Oregon collapse.

It was soon after his time in Crete that he dropped the name Bhagwan Shree Rajneesh and became Osho. In the Japanese Zen tradition, 'Osho' means 'Master', and he also identified with the oceanic, open-ended sound of the name. Yet while he was deciding, he went nameless for many months. With the change of name, his teachings began to focus more on Zen spirituality. They became less physical and celebratory in nature and more inward-focused. He stopped reading the ten books per day he was accustomed to devouring, year after year, instead cultivating the simplicity of 'no-mind.' I like to think he gained some measure of peace.

Yet even at that late stage, Osho wasn't an ascetic guru who urged his followers to give up or deny anything. He wanted them to fully experience the gamut of human emotion, the totality of experience: anger, aggression, happiness, irritation, despair, disappointment, desire, lust, love. At the same time, he urged them to understand that the ultimate aim was to 'work on oneself', to go beyond the personal and reach the impersonal plane, where there is no self. He had a Jungian and Reichian concept of the unconscious mind and implemented many Western psychoanalytical techniques in his 'encounter groups', which were basically an active and confronting form of group therapy. Some people walked away with more trauma than when they started – broken bones, bruises, black eyes, the opening up of old wounds of sexual abuse and childhood neglect. Many mixed-sex groups were undertaken naked, which was challenging for the more inhibited. Yet many felt healed, free, more authentic and on the path to leaving behind the idea of a fixed personality.

Osho also took many of early 20th century Greek-Armenian George Gurdjieff's teachings and translated them into a modern context. The ancient Sufi precepts and Eastern Orthodox mysticism Gurdjieff was steeped in became something wild and transcendent in Osho's teachings. He made use of what Gurdjieff called 'devices' for awakening– practices such as the encounter groups, hard physical labour and deliberately confusing pronouncements. There is a hilarious YouTube video of one of his later talks. A young, female sanyassin asks him why he once spoke about the boundless love of God and now tells her God is dead. He replies with the blend of deadpan humour and compassion he became so famous for. 'Baby,' he says, drowned out by a chorus of laughter from the crowd. 'My whole work is to confuse you.'

In Osho's cosmology, there was no denial of the darkness, shame or vulnerability inherent in the human personality. He also acknowledged the limitations of therapy, instead preferring the term 'psycho-spiritual philosophy' for his techniques. Without meditation, he claimed, therapy only scratched the surface of personality and didn't get to what he termed our 'original face.' Only meditative practices could do that, in tandem with consciously releasing emotion, especially anger and aggression. We can't heal by psychology alone; instead the 'being-ness' or ease of meditation is the bedrock, bringing light to the unconscious. 'Do not swim,' he said. 'Float.'

Many current and former sanyassins told me that looking into Osho's big, irreverent brown eyes was like looking at nobody. There was nobody there. Gazing at him was like gazing into an empty mirror – they only saw their own state of mind reflected back at them. Yet paradoxically, what they did feel emanating from him in great waves was warmth and unconditional love. He saw the entirety of their being, their past, present and future. There was nowhere to hide, and they didn't want to. 'Die each moment so that you can be new in each moment,' he proposed, in his half-serious, tongue-in-cheek version of the Ten Commandments. His epitaph, which he wrote himself before he died, simply said, 'Never born, never died, just visited this earth.' Maybe that's what we need to take away from Osho's story. Live in the present. Die to yourself.

Since living opposite Gondwana in Byron Bay, I've found it a struggle to reconcile Osho's teachings – which make so much sense to me now – with the debacle of Oregon and Rajneeshpuram. How could a supposed enlightened being, even any spiritual teacher much less a guru, allow such crimes to be committed by his closest followers? Since writing Zorba the Buddha I've come to an uneasy appreciation of how this could happen, and how I can still benefit from the teacher while being clear-eyed and critical of the man.

In Osho's own words, 'Being enlightened doesn't mean I know when my bedroom is being bugged.'

Acknowledgements

Katerina Cosgrove is runner-up in the 2020 Carmel Bird Digital Literary Award for *Zorba The Buddha*. The winner of the award is Michalia Arathimos for *Apologia* and fellow runner-up is Brooke Dunnell for *Female(s and) Dogs*. The judge of the 2020 award was Justin Wolfers.

Cover designs for the 2020 series are by Bettina Kaiser

This award is named in honour of renowned Australian author Carmel Bird, who has published a range of short fiction, novels and books on writing and was awarded the Patrick White Award for Literature in 2016.

Launched in 2017, the Carmel Bird Digital Literary Award is an annual competition that showcases new works of short fiction up to 30,000 words in length from Australian writers. It is run by Spineless Wonders and supported by the Copyright Agency's Cultural Fund.

Finalists in the Carmel Bird Digital Literary Award are published electronically by Spineless Wonders.

www.shortaustralianstories.com.au

Praise for Katerina Cosgrove

The Glass Heart

'*The Glass Heart* is a dreaming...sung out of blood and memory and ritual. In prose that is sensual, vivid, savage, frightening and magical, Katerina Cosgrove's novel is a meditation on inheritance that becomes both an invocation and a devotion to the task of remembering.'

Anna Maria Dell'oso

'*The Glass Heart* shimmers with Cosgrove's evocative powers ...Visceral images of eating, drinking, love-making, giving birth and dying are treated with an unerring eye. Cosgrove's writing has beautiful, poetic flourishes so it's not surprising her name has been coupled with the likes of Allende and Garcia Marquez.'

The Age

'Cancel that trip to the Greek islands and read this book instead...this is as real as it gets. It would be difficult to surpass Katerina Cosgrove's intense evocation...

This book will erase your sense of the here and now… Cosgrove does not flinch from offsetting the good with the bad, powerfully rendering the difficulty and rawness…intimately, jaggedly female in its bias, scored with eroticism, pain and loss…this is a captivating read.'

The Australian

'When you read a book that's fantastic it takes – perhaps unfairly – from those around it. And so *The Glass Heart* draws an invisible line around itself that says, this book is special, take it slowly, enjoy it, remember it…The measured prose links past and present with parallels in plot, subtle shifts in imagery and the constant counter-balance of two different lives.'

The Canberra Times

'This is a provocative, sensual telling of relationships and bonds that defy generations…Cosgrove's telling is tantalisingly ripe with the tastes and smells of Greece… Her characters are drawn with honesty and rawness as she digs a finger into the dark and brittle places of the heart.'

The Sunday Mail

'This story teaches us about our world, asking what we want for ourselves and future generations. It tells us it's time to learn from history - not to repeat it'

Dr Izzeldin Abuelaish, author of *I Shall Not Hate*

'A novel that is truly powerful, atmospheric, affecting, shocking yet level-handed. Cosgrove does not take sides, though others will, I suspect. Readers of Orhan Pamuk, Barbara Kingsolver and Tom Keneally will find this a rewarding read.'

Books + Publishing

'*Bone Ash Sky* is a novel of an ambition that is no longer uncommon in Australian fiction, but still remarkable. The interlacing of disparate characters' lives might have been implausible. In Cosgrove's hands it seems fated… For Cosgrove, a Sydney writer with Greek roots who spent a long and fruitful time researching this novel, Bone Ash Sky may seem like the recommencement of her career. It is, in any event, a notable feat of imagination and execution on a scale that never daunted her.'

The Australian

'Cosgrove writes poetically about brutality. Her sentences are sparse and her imagery fierce…Her attempt to cover all sides of the spectrum, the depth of the research and fearlessness in writing about subjects such as the 1915 Armenian genocide - still denied by Turkish scholars - is truly commendable…I was left with a sense that this powerful story is a timely and impassioned plea for a better world, where cross-cultural and inter-religious divides no longer exist.'

The Sydney Morning Herald

'An ambitious, politically charged and terrifically restrained novel.'

Patrick Allington, judging the Writing Australia Unpublished Manuscript Award

'…an incredible novel from a unique talent… Cosgrove's prose is sinuous, pictorial and terrifically controlled…Cosgrove's work seems to have more authority and authenticity because she writes so passionately and serenely.'

In Daily, Adelaide's Independent News

'*Bone Ash Sky* is enlightening, shocking and absorbing.'

Good Reading Magazine

Intimate Distance

Novella, *Griffith Review*

'Katerina Cosgrove's *Intimate Distance* is the longest piece of the collection; a stirring and heartfelt portrayal of one woman's struggle to discover who she is. It details Mara's deeply conflicted love for two brothers, and the aftermath of her life with a child and an ailing mother. With a Turkish-Greek heritage and a father she never knew, Mara leaves her mother in a nursing home and journeys across the seas to where it all began.

In the ancient city of Ephesus, Mara chances upon Zoi, a Greek doctor working in Turkey for a year who she follows back to Athens; an experience that will come to define her and forever change her life. Moving back and forth between Ephesus, Athens, the isolated Greek village of Lithohori, and Sydney, where Mara hails from, Cosgrove's unchronological narrative jumps between 2012, 2013 and 2017, and is vastly effective in charting the protagonist's confused state of jumbled emotions, displacement and disarray.

With its overarching themes of forbidden love, abandonment, filial duty versus individual needs, and unresolved passion, *Intimate Distance* effectively delves into the dichotomy between the individualistic societies of the West and the more family-oriented, collective societies of Greece, where Mara simultaneously flounders and finds her very reason for being.'

ArtsHub

'A tale of infidelity and parenthood…Cosgrove's loving depiction of the Greek setting and her sophisticated craftsmanship help ground the controversial motherhood-parenthood theme.'

The Sydney Morning Herald

Zorba The Buddha

'This novella is a feat of language – lyrical, intricate, sensory. A collision of raw power and manipulation with storytelling as art. Every piece wisely and deliberately placed.'

Anna Spargo-Ryan

'Cosgrove has braided a vibrant tapestry of a guru fallen from grace, as she delves into the final days of Osho, passing the mic from the guiltless to the guilty, from believer to sinner. This entangling web of voices throws up unexpected shadows and a slithery truth. A stirring portrayal by an astonishing storyteller who doesn't settle for easy resolutions.'

Joanne Fedler

'Cosgrove's deceptively slim book is in fact a tightly packed cornucopia of literary delights – careful character studies, dark intrigues, and stunning prose, all threaded through with a philosophical contemplation of how best to live our lives. Zorba The Buddha is an urgent, riveting work from an accomplished storyteller. A feat of a book!'

Lee Kofman

Biography

Katerina Cosgrove has co-owned café-bookshops (Sappho Books, Gertrude & Alice) and taught at the University of Technology, Sydney, where she gained her BA (Honours) and Doctorate in Creative Arts (Australian Postgraduate Award). She is the author of two novels, The Glass Heart (HarperCollins), *Bone Ash Sky* (Hardie Grant) and prize-winning short stories. *Bone Ash Sky* was a finalist for the Writing Australia Unpublished Manuscript Award.

Katerina's novella, *Intimate Distance* (Text) won the Griffith Review Novella Prize. She has appeared on SBS, ABC and BBC TV, radio and written for Al-Jazeera, *The Independent*, *The Age*, *The Sydney Morning Herald*, SBS *Voices*, *Island*, *The Australian*, *Australian Author*, *Daily Life*, *The Big Issue*, *The Huffington Post*, *Culture Trip*, *Audrey*, *Dumbo Feather* and many other publications, as well as published in prose and poetry anthologies.

Her work has been translated into Greek, Spanish, French, Armenian, Chinese, Korean and Italian and made into podcasts. Katerina has been the recipient of Australia Council grants and residencies in Australia and overseas. She has been co-judging the Mark and Evette Moran Nib Award for Literature from 2014 and the Australia reMADE poetry competition in 2019. Katerina also writes obituaries through her site www.livelifetwice.com.

Visit www.facebook.com/AuthorCosgrove, Twitter @ katcosgrove, or Katerina's website www.katerinacosgrove.com

About This Series

Zorba The Buddha by Katerina Cosgrove is published as part of the Spineless Wonders Smalls series of small format paperbacks released to celebrate our tenth year in publishing.

To find out about other books published in this series, go to www.shortaustralianstories.com.au

www.shortaustralianstories.com.au